Pride Publishing books by Thom Collins

Anthem
Anthem of the Sea

Anthologies
Brothers in Arms

I0542415

Anthem

ANTHEM OF THE DARK

THOM COLLINS

Anthem of the Dark
ISBN # 978-1-78686-380-5
©Copyright Thom Collins 2018
Cover Art by Cherith Vaughn ©Copyright September 2018
Interior text design by Claire Siemaszkiewicz
Pride Publishing

Published in 2018 by Pride Publishing, United Kingdom.

Pride Publishing is an imprint of Totally Entwined Group Limited.

ANTHEM OF
THE DARK

Dedication

For my husband, Liam

Prologue

Article from the Bournemouth Chronicle, 25th July

Former Popstar Murdered in Bungled Robbery.

Local businessman and one-time pop singer, Luke Torrens, thirty-two, has been killed in an attempted robbery on his store, Surf's Up, in Bournemouth. Mr. Torrens, who owned the surfing supply store since 2012, was pronounced dead at the scene. He was discovered by a customer shortly after opening the shop on Saturday morning. Police have appealed for anyone in the area at that time to contact them.

Mr. Torrens was formerly a member of the defunct boy band Overload, which launched the career of The One *star Daniel Blake. In recent years, Mr. Torrens shunned the limelight in favor of a settled family life by the sea, while Daniel achieved national fame in TV and music.*

He leaves behind a wife and two children.

Chapter One

The audience rose to their feet and applauded. The entire auditorium went crazy. Standing in the wings, waiting to take his curtain call, Daniel Blake couldn't hold back his smile. Blackpool Opera House had a capacity of almost three thousand people, and everyone there showed their appreciation. The noise was deafening as the company and supporting players took their bows.

Nothing could equal this. It was electric.

For two and a half hours, the cast had kept the audience enthralled. They were on the second performance of the day, but the energy level never faltered. Everyone involved in the show, front and backstage, was at the top of their game. The crowd had reacted and laughed in all the right places.

With everyone back on stage except the two star players, the applause reached a new peak of excitement. On the opposite wing, waiting for her cue, stood Daniel's co-star, Max LaFranchi. She flashed a megawatt smile and gave an excited thumbs-up. Max had been entertaining audiences since she was twelve, and standing ovations were nothing new to her, but even she appeared wowed by this response.

She gave Daniel the nod, and they entered the stage from their opposite sides. The noise came out of the auditorium in waves at a near-deafening level. They met in the center before taking each other's hand and walking to the front. The excitement was palpable.

"Wow," Daniel gasped. Seven weeks into a two-month run and the audience reaction hadn't faltered. Night after night it had maintained the same level. In all his career, he hadn't experienced such a definite hit.

He lost track of time as the curtain came down, only to rise again moments later. The applause seemed endless and when the curtain dropped for the last time the euphoria didn't die with it.

"Can you believe it?" he said to Max. Cast and crew scurried around them, eager to be done now the show was over.

She laughed. "There are no words for *that*. It was just…incredible."

Max LaFranchi was show business through and through. A former child star turned theatrical diva. Now fifty-four, her passion for the stage and the audience remained undimmed.

The staggering success of *Lady Lynda* had taken everyone by surprise. Launching an original show was always a gamble. More so in these days of jukebox musicals and movie-to-stage adaptions. The script was a winner, hilarious and poignant by turn, and the songs were immediately catchy, but it was still a major risk. Too much so for the producers to chance launching it in London, even with the pulling power of two big name leads. A summer in Blackpool was a means to trial the show away from the harsh eyes of London critics. To discover what worked and what didn't and make the necessary changes.

But from the preview shows in July, scarcely a word had been altered.

The audiences had loved it from the start and the entire run had sold out.

"Won't you change your mind and come on the town with us?" Max asked. "It won't be the same without you. We've had such a great evening, don't let it end."

"Not tonight," he replied. "You know I can't."

"Oh, c'mon. Blackpool and all it offers, you love it. Don't we always have a ball?"

Daniel laughed. "You know I do. But not tonight. I'm going home straight from the theater."

With no show scheduled for Sunday, he wasn't due back on stage until Monday evening. And Daniel had a good reason to go home, the best reason — Elijah. His lover and soulmate. The only man who mattered. They hadn't seen each other for two weeks and it felt like a lifetime. Skype and FaceTime didn't cut it. Daniel had to see him in the flesh. To hold him and kiss him, stroke his hair and breathe in the smell of him. He'd go mad if he had to wait much longer.

Max pouted. "Everyone is coming out tonight. Can't you stay for an hour?"

He put his arm around her slender shoulder. "Max, I love you, but not as much as Elijah. Nothing is gonna keep me from him tonight. Not even you."

"Fair enough," she said. "I know what it's like to be that much in love. Though God knows it's been a bloody long time for me. I'm on the verge of becoming a nun."

"You wouldn't last five minutes. I don't think they allow champagne in the Abbey."

"Then I'm never becoming a nun. All right, if you won't come out with us, stop by my room before you take off. We'll have a glass of champagne."

"I'm driving."

"Half a glass then. And that's final. Not another word of protest."

Daniel hurried to his dressing room. He would have to be quick. He didn't want to offend Max, but he needed to be on the road as soon as possible. Elijah was already waiting. He'd texted earlier to let Daniel know he'd arrived home safely. Daniel couldn't wait to get there. Since the show had begun, they'd seen each other at least once a week, but work commitments for Elijah had kept him away last weekend. Daniel had stayed in Blackpool rather than go home to an empty house.

He was a realist. They were entertainers and traveling was part of the job, but he hated the time they spent apart. Seeing each other once or twice a week was enough. It gave him something to look forward to. But these last two weeks had been too long—all he'd been able to think about was tonight.

Joe, his wardrobe assistant, stood alert in the dressing room when Daniel entered. He'd argued that he didn't need help to put his clothes on, but *Lady Lynda* was set in the 1920s and a hell of a lot of money had gone into the costumes. It was Joe's job to look after the clothes and make sure he didn't ruin them.

"Another great night." Joe grinned, hanging up his jacket. At twenty, Joe had lived in Blackpool all his life, giving him a strong regional accent. Joe was slim with a crown of dirty blond hair. He had a wide mouth with cupid-bow lips and the most intensely colored olive-green eyes. Kind of cute but not Daniel's type. Too young for a start. Besides, no man compared with Elijah.

"This is it then," Daniel said. "We're into the final week. I'll be sad when it ends next Saturday, won't you?"

"Big time. But it's not all doom and gloom, is it? We've got the wrap party. I'm looking forward to it."

"I *knew* you were a party boy," Daniel joked, unbuttoning his shirt.

"I'm a Blackpool boy." Joe chuckled, running fingers through his thick hair. "Partying is in the blood. Just wait and see. Once I get a few beers down, there's no stopping me. Will your fella be coming to the party?"

"Certainly."

"Even better. We've all missed him this week. I like Elijah. He's a good laugh."

Daniel stripped to his underpants and gave the clothes back to Joe. Backstage in a theater was no place for modesty. Joe had seen it all before.

Daniel sat at the mirror and carefully extracted the microphone wires concealed in his hair, then set about cleaning off the stage makeup. Makeup was all part of the job, but what a relief to wipe it off. Clean at last, he gazed at his bare reflection.

Two shows in one day could take a toll and he often came off stage exhausted. But not tonight. With the exuberance of the curtain call and the anticipation of seeing Elijah, Daniel's sky-blue eyes were luminous.

Daniel's looks had played a massive part in the success of *Lady Lynda*. His square jaw, with its cowboy cleft and his sharp cheek bones, were traditionally handsome in appearance. His matinee idol image suited the old-fashioned style of the show.

Daniel brushed his dark brown hair off his forehead and set about dressing. He drew on a pair of jeans and a black T-shirt, clean socks and shoved his feet into a trusty pair of Converse shoes. He was good to go.

Five minutes with Max, then he was out of here.

As he headed to her dressing room, one of the backstage assistants rushed toward him.

"There's quite a crowd at the stage door," the man told him. "They all want to meet you."

"Okay."

He would greet the fans before seeing Max. Some of them had to face a long journey home and he didn't want to keep them waiting.

Another round of applause erupted as he stepped out of the door. Daniel smiled widely at the people waiting. There looked to be around fifty. *Oh boy, this'll take some time.* He wouldn't complain, but of all the times to get delayed at the theater, why did it have to be tonight? He loved his fans, people paid a lot of money to see the show, but all he wanted, right now was Elijah.

The people waiting had already organized themselves into a queue.

"Thanks for coming, everyone," he shouted down the line. "It's amazing to see so many happy faces. Did you all have a good night?"

They cheered their response.

He signed autographs and posed for photos. A lot of actors were sniffy about meeting people at the stage door and often tried to find an alternative route out of the theater. Daniel had no time for such pretensions. He could only do this job because people bought tickets to see him.

"When is the show going to open in London?" asked an ardent woman in her early fifties.

"There's nothing set in stone," he answered, signing her program. "Hopefully around Christmas, or early next year."

"You'll be going with it, won't you?"

"I hope so," he said, "but it all depends on when and where it happens."

"But you *have* to," she asserted. "It won't be the same without you."

"Thanks for saying so. Hopefully it will all work out. I can't say for definite, but if I *can* do it, I will."

The line moved slowly. He made time for everyone but signing all those programs and posing for selfies was no quick job. They were the usual blend of people—a mix of middle-aged housewives and gays, tipsy girls on a night out and shy kids.

"So lovely to see you on top form again," a woman with a Liverpool accent told him. "We were so worried after what happened to you on that cruise ship. We heard you nearly died."

Daniel smiled, though it was a little forced. "It's ancient history. Exaggerated history at that. I've put it all behind me. I'm glad you liked the show."

Not that ancient. Less than a year had passed since that fateful voyage on *The Atlantic Anthem*. Some days, it felt much less than that.

He finally reached the end of the line, though the crowd were in no hurry to leave.

"Will Max be coming out soon?" a well-dressed older guy asked.

"I'll get her for you," he said, slipping back inside. Duty done. If he came out behind Max, he could get away while she distracted the fans.

Loud music came from her dressing room. He recognized it as a song from the show, though it had been given an over-the-top dance remix. Daniel knocked and entered.

Inside, it was crowded. She had the biggest room in the theater, but with a dozen people jammed in and flowers on every surface, there was no space to spare.

Max had taken off her costume and removed her wig. She was brushing her shoulder-length, coppery-gold hair when she caught his reflection in the mirror.

"Daniel, come in. Listen to this. Isn't it fabulous?"

Max's big number in the show was a song called *Roses and Raindrops*. The original version was bombastic and camp, a big-diva moment at the end of act one. This remixed version sent the song into the stratosphere.

"What the hell is this?" He laughed.

"We've had it reworked as a single for the clubs," she said. "Can you believe it? I'm going to be a disco diva. Me, fifty-four years old and four-foot-six, camping it up in the clubs."

"I can't believe you haven't done it before."

"I know, right? It's insane. So, c'mon, what do you think?"

"The gays are gonna to love it."

"But what about you?"

He threw open his hands. "Totally jealous," he exaggerated.

Max threw back her head and roared. "We'll have to get some of your songs jazzed up too. We could do a whole album. *Lady Lynda: The Remixes*. Have some champagne."

"Just a half, remember." He helped himself to a spare glass and half-filled it. "You need to get dressed. There's a crowd outside and they're not going anywhere until they meet you."

"We'll go out together," she said, applying blood-red lipstick.

"I've already done my part. They're all yours."

"Spoilsport. Are you positive you don't want to come out with us? You can have my driver, he'll take you home at the end of the night. All the way to Elijah's arms."

Daniel slowly shook his head. Typical Max, she was always trying to make mischief. "No means no," he said firmly. "My man is waiting at home and I intend to spend the night with him. Not gallivanting around Blackpool with a wannabe disco diva."

"I'm no wannabe. When I do something, I do it heart and soul." She stood up and slipped behind a dressing screen. "Why can't Elijah come here? We could all go out together. I haven't seen him in ages."

"He's coming next weekend. But tonight, it's just the two of us. You can't have him."

"Take no notice of me," she said. "I'm just jealous. If I had a hot guy to go home to, I wouldn't be tramping around town on a Saturday night, either."

She came back from behind the screen wearing slim-fitting black pants and a sheer black top. Even in her towering heels, Max LaFranchi was tiny. She had the petite figure of a young girl. She crossed back to the dressing table and began layering on gold chains and bangles.

"Maybe there's a hot guy out there waiting to meet you," Daniel said.

"What? Here? In Blackpool? Not likely. The guys who talk to me are all drunk or gay. More often than not, both."

"Love turns up when you least expect it." That was certainly true. With everything that had happened on *The Atlantic Anthem*, the last thing Daniel had expected was to fall in love.

"All right," Max said, checking her appearance one last time. "Let's do this."

As predicted, when she tottered out of the stage door, the whole crowd rushed to meet her. Daniel moved to the edge and slipped away unnoticed. *Eleven-fifty. Not too bad.* The traffic home to Leeds would be light. With a little luck, he'd make it in an hour.

There were butterflies in his stomach as he hastened to his car.

He was going home to Elijah. He'd be there soon.

Daniel couldn't wait.

Chapter Two

It had gone midnight. Not long to wait.

Elijah Mann took a bottle of champagne from the fridge and pushed it into an ice bucket beside two crystal flutes. He loaded a bowl with pitted olives, which he had seasoned with lemon and fresh coriander, and laid out a small platter of cured meats and cheeses. It was a simple but delicious late supper. The last thing he wanted to do tonight was cook. He'd spent the past two months working in a variety of kitchens — now he was home, he planned to relax. At least for tonight.

It had been a long evening on his own. The wait for Daniel was interminable.

The house they shared in Horsforth, Leeds was perfect in just about every way. Compact and modern, it was big enough for two men to live by side without crowding each other, with a location close to the city, the railway station and the motorway. Wherever their work demanded, they could be on their way in less than ten minutes. The property was set back from the main road behind a ten-foot wall. Privacy was never a problem despite its proximity to the city. The house had everything.

But tonight, it missed one vital element—Daniel. Without him, it was just an empty house.

Elijah had arrived home around seven after a busy train service from Edinburgh. The emptiness was evident the moment he walked through the door. Daniel had been away for as long as he had, close to two weeks, and the house had taken on the quiet air of desolation that happens when a building stays empty. Their cleaner had been in to deal with the laundry and dusting, but it wasn't the same as when they lived here.

He'd gone around turning on lights, closing curtains, burning candles, seeking to bring warmth and atmosphere back to the place. He put on some music to kill the silence.

Elijah had moved in just before Christmas. To family and friends, it looked as if they were moving too fast. They had only known each other two months, but after what happened on the *Atlantic*, they'd had an accelerated courtship. When the ship had returned to Southampton, Daniel had been rushed straight to hospital. The knife Oliver Gill had stuck in his side had perforated his large intestine. The ship's medics had kept him stable, but they'd had no time to waste. He'd needed surgery, fast. Thankfully the knife had missed his major organs. Elijah had barely left his side as he recuperated. Even now he found it hard to be away from him. The physical scars had healed but the emotional damage Oliver had caused lingered.

Daniel's career had exploded after the news broke.

Daniel Blake — TV star, talent show champion and the nation's favorite-boy-next-door — had narrowly escaped an attempt on his life. Everyone wanted a piece of him. TV, radio and newspapers — the requests for interviews were endless. He was in demand. There were new record deals on offer, book contracts, West End shows and soap operas.

In the beginning, Daniel had wanted none of it. Shunning the world, he'd retreated behind the walls of the house. Elijah had done everything to support him but it hadn't been easy. The healing process had taken a long time. Elijah regularly woke to find Daniel tossing back and forth, in the throes of a nightmare, his side of the bed awash with sweat as his dreams transported him back to the *Anthem*. Elijah couldn't do anything but hold him and reassure him it was over.

Oliver was dead. His body had been pulled from the dark water of the Atlantic Ocean in the early hours — he couldn't hurt them now.

Elijah checked the time again and crossed to the window. The narrow drive was lit by the orange flame of a street lamp on the other side of their wall. Still no sign of Daniel.

"Hurry up, babe," he whispered.

Stop worrying. Daniel can take care of himself.

All the same, Elijah wouldn't relax until he was home.

Elijah's career had also skyrocketed in the aftermath of the *Anthem*. Before that he'd struggled to secure many bookings on the comedy circuit. His once-promising TV profile had been close to extinction. Now he was in demand again. Doors that had been closed before stood wide open.

He'd found it repugnant at first, that his career should thrive because of his association with a psychopath. A

man who'd murdered his friend and tried to kill his boyfriend. Like Daniel, he'd resisted the offers that came in. He wanted to succeed on talent, not notoriety.

At the start of the year, he'd had a shift in attitude. The press had still been desperate to hear his version of the story. A lot of people from the *Anthem* had taken the opportunity to raise their profile and put their stories out there. Terry St. King had accomplished a tremendous career renaissance. He even toured the UK, selling out theaters and city halls, thanks to his connection with Oliver Gill and Daniel. Passengers and crew members leaped on the bandwagon. Those with the most tenuous link to the drama had a story to sell.

Elijah hated it. It had pissed him off that one story went untold. One voice went unheard.

Anouska Frost. His friend. The woman who'd gotten in Oliver's way when he was set on destroying Daniel. Anouska had suffered more than anyone and had paid with her life.

But no one wanted her story.

After several months, he'd found it infuriating. Aggravating.

'It's like they've forgotten her. The girl died and all anyone cares about are petty scandals.'

'Why don't you do something about it?' Daniel had said.

'I will.'

Having turned down all previous requests for an interview, Elijah had finally relented. He'd agreed to a sit-down, face-to-face discussion on a prime-time current affairs show, on one condition—that he told Anouska's story.

'She was my friend. I won't let her be forgotten.'

True to his word, when the interviewer had deviated and asked about his relationship with Daniel, he had ignored the question and brought it right back to the subject that mattered. Anouska.

It was a catharsis that had allowed him to move on. He began to consider some of the offers he received but rejected everything that came with a personal angle. He refused to talk about the *Anthem*, about Daniel or what had really happened been him and Oliver. He got back into comedy. His first TV appearance after the Anouska interview was an eight-minute stand-up routine on Friday night TV. It had terrified him, like a novice stepping up for his first open-mic gig. His fears were baseless. He'd smashed the performance and people remembered he was a funny man, a comedian, and not just a player in a tragedy at sea.

'I told you, you'd ace it.' Daniel hugged him in the green room afterward.

It was a turning point for both of them. Time to live again. They had to go back to work.

For the first time in his career, Elijah had choices. Prior to this he'd accepted any work he was offered. Now he could be selective. Comedy, presenting, acting — the offers came from all directions. He'd even landed a couple of modelling gigs. *Modeling*. It was insane. But the photographs proved otherwise. In a series of moody black and white shots, he'd appeared in a stack of glossy men's mags fronting a campaign for a high-street fashion chain. Elijah had never been a vain man. He knew he wasn't ugly. Some had suggested in the past he was too good-looking to be funny as a comedian. Those underhand comments were flattering in a way, though he never took them seriously. But the photos were something else. He looked like a Hollywood star. An old-fashioned dreamboat.

Almost as handsome as Daniel.

Celebrity Top Cook had always been one of his favorite programs. A prime-time TV show in which a bunch of familiar faces competed for the title of top chef. It was a mainstay of the TV schedules when it aired each autumn — a well-done family favorite that continually drew audience figures of five million plus. He couldn't believe it when his agent called him with an offer to appear on the next series.

"You love that show," Daniel said. "Why not do it?"

"I'm not a *celebrity*," he protested.

"But you are. They wouldn't ask you otherwise. I'll bet you're more famous than most of the other contestants."

"I can't cook either."

"Sure you can. You do a mean chicken curry. And you're half Greek. What about all those family recipes your mother taught you? You're perfect for this."

"It'll take more than a basic stew to get ahead in this show."

Despite his doubts, he took the offer. It was *Celebrity Top Cook*, for heaven's sake. He'd be a mug to turn it down. What was the worst that could happen? That he'd be ousted in the first round of the competition. So what? The experience would make it worthwhile. How many people were given the chance to take part in their favorite TV show?

After weeks of competition, against all expectations, Elijah had made it to the final three contestants.

Through taking part, he'd discovered a previously untapped skill and passion for cookery. He'd always dabbled in the kitchen when he had time but had a limited culinary repertoire. Like most people, he'd mastered half a dozen core dishes he returned to again and again. Chili, bolognaise, chicken, roast beef, seared salmon and sausages. The show had opened up a new world of cooking—dishes and ingredients he would never have considered before. It had been a revelation.

At each stage of the competition he'd expected to be the next person out and was astonished to make it through. It had been a long and exhausting process, but it was almost over. He had made it to the final. On Monday, they would film the last round of challenges that would lead to the announcement of the winner.

The end was near and his attitude had shifted. Taking part wasn't enough—he had a hunger for success. He wanted the title.

He wanted to win.

Elijah's reverie was broken by a noise outside. The front gate creaked as it swung open. At the same time, the automatic security light flooded the driveway.

Daniel was home.

Elijah rushed to the door and turned the key. Every part of him ached for his man. He knew the unease that had dogged him all evening was pure heartsickness.

Daniel stepped out of car with a wide smile. Elijah ran at him, open armed, and gathered him tight to breathe in his familiar smell.

"God, I've missed you," he said, squeezing the familiar shape of his body. He didn't want to let go.

Daniel turned his head for a kiss. "I've missed you too. So much."

The kiss was long and deep. Daniel's lips were soft, while the roughness of his unshaved chin scratched against Elijah's beard. Elijah put a hand on the back of Daniel's head, drawing him deeper into the kiss. His senses were overwhelmed by the sight of him, the smell of his hair and skin and the hardness of his body, by the strength of his emotions.

"I love you. God, I've missed you so much."

They stood on the drive, holding each other, oblivious to the cold or how late it had gotten. Their world was each other.

"Let's go inside." Elijah put a hand around Daniel's waist and drew him toward the house. "You must be tired. Tough drive?"

"Not at all," Daniel said, settling his palm on the curve of Elijah's butt. "How could I be tired now I'm here? It's been a long two weeks."

"I know," Elijah said, locking the door behind them and guiding Daniel to the kitchen. "It couldn't be helped. Not when we're working."

"I know. But it doesn't mean I have to like it."

"You're here now. Let's just enjoy it."

He took a step back to look at Daniel properly. There were no signs that he'd performed two high-powered shows that day and driven cross-country to get here after midnight. His blue eyes were dazzlingly bright, while his skin had a flawless, incandescent glow. And his smile. In all the time they'd known each other, it had lost none of its impact. Elijah would have walked all the way to Blackpool just to see it.

"You look gorgeous. They've been taking care of you."

Daniel chuckled. "Not as well as you do. And now you're a *Top Cook* finalist I expect you to spoil me a whole lot more. You were already sexy and funny, but now you can cook. That's a triple threat."

"Sorry to disappoint, but tonight I'm cooked out." Elijah gestured toward the platter of cured meats and olives. "This is all I could rustle up. It's not too late to order a pizza, if you want something hot instead."

"You're all I want," Daniel said, leaning forward for another kiss.

"That's something you can have for free," Elijah replied, succumbing to his lips.

Daniel eventually drew back. "I must stink. I left the theater without taking a shower."

"You smell great to me," Elijah said, pouring two glasses of champagne.

They raised their glassed and clinked. "Cheers."

"How was Spain?" Daniel asked.

As the competition had heated up toward the end, the final five contestants of *Celebrity Top Cook* had traveled to Spain for a week of intense challenges. Elijah had worked a busy evening shift in a tapas bar in Malaga, cooking a variety of local specialties for the hungry customers and the celebrity judges. After that there had been a group challenge when the five opponents had to work as a single unit, preparing a five-course meal for a party of local dignitaries.

"The best thing I've done in my whole career," he said. "Truly out of this world. I had no idea I would take to working in a professional kitchen quite so easily. I loved it. The pressure, the standards, the sense of achievement when you send out a plate of food and people tell you how much they love it."

Daniel grinned and helped himself to a slice of chorizo from the platter. "Maybe you missed your true vocation."

Elijah shrugged. "That has crossed my mind. I've always enjoyed pottering about in a kitchen, but that's all it's ever been — pottering. But now, I've got a passion to learn about different food and cultures, about ingredients and techniques."

"There's nothing to stop you if you really want to do that. You can do anything. I'm glad you agreed to go on the show. I haven't seen you this excited about work since…"

"Since the *Anthem*?"

Daniel nodded. "You know, I was averse to going back to work myself. It would have been easy to stay here and hide behind the gates. But we needed to get out. Both of us. And it's done us good, don't you think?"

Elijah put down his glass and shifted closer. He slid his hands around Daniel's waist and brought his hips against his. "It has. It's done us a lot of good." He kissed him again, slowly, savoring each sensation.

Daniel responded. The hardness in his front of his trousers was obvious. He ground the bulge against Elijah's hips.

"Let's go upstairs."

* * * *

Hot water spurted from powerful shower jets and coursed over their hard, naked bodies. Standing directly beneath the faucet, they were locked at the mouth, their tongues driving back and forth. Elijah gripped Daniel's hot, soapy arse in both hands and kept their hips pressed tight against each other. Their cocks rubbed together in the slickness between them.

God, he had missed this.

Daniel moaned, breaking the kiss to press his mouth against Elijah's shoulder. Despite the heat of the water, his skin broke into gooseflesh as Daniel's tongue flicked across his neck. Elijah's cock throbbed. He'd left it alone all week, saving himself for tonight, for Daniel. His balls ached for release.

"I want you," he groaned, pushing his fingers between Daniel's buttocks and probing the wet, hairy crack. They've been together long enough to know every inch of each other's body. Every intimacy. Elijah knew exactly how to drive Daniel crazy. He found the opening hot and responsive. Daniel nipped the nape of Elijah's neck as the tip of his index finger entered him. *So tight, so smooth.* Elijah pressed deeper.

"Yes," Daniel hissed, digging his fingers into the muscle of Elijah's shoulders.

"Is that what you want?" he teased, going farther.

Daniel rocked his hips against his hand. "Fuck me."

"Really?"

He found the smooth curve of Daniel's prostate and gently stroked it. The lightest touch, barely any pressure.

Daniel responded, widening his thighs, holding Elijah tighter, giving up his arse.

"Oh, God. That's intense. Fuck me."

Elijah loved his passionate plea.

He spun Daniel around, pressing him against the door of the shower. He grasped Daniel's hips, holding him in place, and gently nibbled the flesh of his shoulder. Daniel's entire body shuddered. Elijah nudged his legs apart. Daniel widened his feet, giving him fuller access. Elijah pressed the wet tip of his cock into the cleft, rubbing it up and down the slippery passage, teasing his hole. Then he paused, scarcely touching, staying out of reach.

Daniel extended his stance, pushing his hips back farther. "C'mon, stop teasing. I want it."

"This?" Elijah whispered, twitching his cock, letting it sweep up and down the crack.

"Yes," Daniel pleaded. "Do it."

Despite enjoying the game, Elijah only had so much restraint. His own desire drove him crazy. He thrust his cock into the crack. The water, together with the willingness of their bodies, made it effortless.

"Oh, God," they groaned together.

Elijah pushed all the way and Daniel took it. He wrapped his hands around Daniel's belly, holding their bodies close. He pressed his lips against Daniel's ear.

"I love you," he said, thrusting.

There was an urgency for both of them. They'd have the rest of the weekend to make love—right now, they needed to fuck. They ground their bodies together in the wet, steamy confines of the cubicle. Skin smacked against skin. The sound reverberated through the bathroom. Daniel turned his head sideways, mouth and tongue searching for Elijah, while he ground his arse against him.

They timed it to perfection. Attuned to each other's rhythms, Daniel squirted his thick, white seed across the glass as Elijah's orgasm tore through his body. Elijah gripped him tight, holding him upright while they rode the waves of ecstasy.

They were together again in every way.

Chapter Three

Daniel awoke slowly as bright sunlight penetrated the curtains. Elijah was in the kitchen downstairs, singing along to love songs on the radio. He rolled over and raised his head, blinking the bedside clock into focus. It had gone eleven. Late, even by his own Sunday standards.

He always slept well when he was home.

He couldn't grumble about the accommodation in Blackpool. Both he and Max were staying at the best hotel in town with suites, king-sized beds and twenty-four-hour room service. But a hotel, no matter how fancy, was still a hotel and couldn't compete with the pleasures of home. Especially not for a homeboy like him.

He stretched languorously and pressed his spine into the mattress. No, nothing could beat his own bed.

He couldn't remember what time they had turned in last night, but it had been late — it had to have been. After fucking hard and fast in the shower, they'd climbed into bed to finish the champagne. They had talked for a long time, catching up on each other's news and sharing gossip from work. They had made love again before turning out the lights, long and soft, holding each other and kissing throughout. The last thing he remembered as he had drifted off to sleep were Elijah's arms around him, his body pressed into the curve of his spine.

Daniel had slept more soundly than he had in weeks.

Things were getting better for him, especially at night. The nightmares that had plagued him since the *Anthem* were less frequent. He still had dreams about Oliver Gill, but they no longer scared him. In the nightmares, Oliver used to appear with crazy eyes and a manic expression — sometimes he wielded a knife, sometimes an axe, but he was always hell-bent on violence. Now, when Daniel dreamed about him, he was a quieter figure, haunted and sad.

He'd be happier when the dreams ceased all together, when he stopped reliving that night at sea, over and over. Until then, Oliver would still be there, exerting a hold from the grave.

Somehow, he had to break it.

Going back to work had been a step in the right direction, massively so, for Elijah and himself. Elijah's accomplishments on *Top Cook* had surprised them both to discover he had such a talent in the kitchen. He deserved the success. He'd earned it. Daniel was so proud of him.

Elijah had persuaded him to take the role in *Lady Lynda*.

When the offer first came, Daniel had wanted to say no. He hadn't been ready to go back to work. The challenge was too big. Overwhelming. The male lead in a brand-new musical. He hadn't thought he had the strength for such a major role. Elijah had convinced him otherwise.

'*It's perfect and you know it,*' he'd said after reading the script for the first time. They had been in the kitchen, listening to a rough demo of the songs for the show. '*I can't think of anyone better. This could have been written for you.*'

'*But it's a big part,*' Daniel had said uncertainly. '*There's so much to learn. Not just the script and the songs, there'll be dance routines and everything that goes with it.*'

'*So? You love all that stuff. It's what you do best, isn't it?*'

'*It used to be. I don't think I have it in me anymore. And the pressure of launching a new show, I don't want that. If it flops, it'll be my fault.*'

'*Rubbish. You're sharing the bill with Max LaFranchi. The queen of musical theatre. There's no way it will flop. The show could be shit and the two of you will still fill the theatre. And it isn't shit. Far from it. It's brilliant. You can't lose.*'

* * * *

Elijah was right, but that hadn't made it easy when Daniel signed on board. He'd never been so anxious about anything in his career. The day he joined the company he was physically sick. He'd been a professional performer since he was sixteen but none of it mattered. His nerves were shot. On the first morning, he'd wanted to pull out.

Max convinced him otherwise. "You've had a bad time," she said in a quiet moment, away from the rest of the cast. "In this business, you have to get used to them. I've been knocked down more times than I can remember, but I got up and started again. That's what you have to do now."

"I don't think I *can* do it. Not anymore," he said.

"Bullshit. You can't see it yourself just now, but I see it in you. I've been around long enough to recognize when somebody's got it, or they haven't. You're the same as me. You *need* this. You need the work. Something to do. All you lack is faith in yourself and this show will give you that."

She was right. Each day of rehearsal was better than the last. The fear slowly waned to be replaced by something else — excitement. When opening night came around, he felt like a champion again.

The specter of Oliver continued to cast a shadow, but its power had receded.

Hoping to lay the ghost to rest for good, Daniel visited his grave. Oliver had grown up in Blackpool and was buried at a cemetery in Lytham St. Anne's. *Lady Lynda* had been running for three weeks when he decided it was time. He went alone one morning when he had nothing else scheduled. It rained for the first time in weeks as he stood before the modest headstone. *Oliver Gill*, it read, *beloved son and brother. Rest easy.* Daniel had had no contact with Oliver's family. He'd read in a newspaper that his mother had died abroad while his sister worked in London. Oliver's social media accounts had been deactivated after his death. Daniel had spent some time looking through the messages and contacts before they were deleted. There wasn't much to see. No family. Few friends.

No one had seemed to miss him.

Nobody cared.

Daniel almost felt sorry for him. In the end, he'd stopped looking.

The past was better forgotten by everyone.

He'd hoped visiting the grave might bring him closure. It didn't. His feelings about Oliver were difficult to pin down. In the nightmares, they manifested as fear but in the day, they varied wildly between anger and sadness. Sometimes he felt nothing. No anger. No grief. Zilch.

Standing over the grave, he waited for a rush of emotions to envelope him. They must surely come, standing with Oliver beneath his feet. Anger, dread, anxiety, relief — there had been something still to come out. But as he lingered in the rain, he realized there was nothing.

Maybe it was for the best.

Better than the alternative.

* * * *

Daniel swung back the bed covers. He'd lain here long enough. Wasting time. He went to the bathroom to relive himself and flattened down his bed-crazy hair. Elijah had seen him at his worst, but that didn't mean he shouldn't make an effort. He put on a clean T-shirt and a pair of pajama shorts before going downstairs.

The most delicious smells issued from the kitchen — coffee and bacon — while Elijah sang along to Dolly Parton on the radio.

"Hello, cowboy," Daniel said, wandering in.

"Hello, sleepyhead." Elijah stood at the counter, chopping an array of vegetables, most of which Daniel didn't recognize. He looked hot as hell in an old pair of shorts that clung to the mounds of his arse, and an ancient red T-shirt. His feet were bare and his freshly washed hair hung loose over his forehead. He looked irresistible. And highly fuckable.

Daniel couldn't stop thinking about sex. They had spent too long apart.

"What are you up to?"

"Practicing. A little something I've thought up for the final."

"What is it?"

"You'll find out later. You need to eat breakfast before you think about dinner. Sit."

Daniel took a seat at the breakfast bar and Elijah brought him orange juice and the pot of coffee. He leaned in for a warm kiss before pouring.

"You're spoiling me," Daniel said, grinning

"I haven't begun." Elijah brushed up close to him. "It's good to be back, isn't it? Just the two of us. No maids, no hotel staff, no intrusions."

Still sitting, Daniel leaned his head into his chest. "Mmm. Have you had any thoughts about next week? About what we could do?"

Lady Lynda had one week left to run in Blackpool, and neither of them had any immediate work lined up. When the show was over, they could make time for each other.

That had been the agreement from the start.

"I just want to be with you," Elijah said.

"What about a holiday? We could book something this week. It's not too late."

Elijah shrugged. "How about we have a few days at home first? A little down time before running off again."

"That sounds perfect."

Elijah moved to the oven. He took out an enormous plate of bacon that he'd been keeping warm, together with grilled mushroom and bread rolls.

"Are you trying to make me fat?" Daniel gasped at the amount of food he brought to the counter.

"No, just build your strength up," he said, fixing him a huge bacon and mushroom roll with a lashing of ketchup, just the way Daniel liked it. "Now eat."

"Yes, boss."

Daniel tucked in. Despite the portion size the food tasted terrific. He'd cooked the bacon to crispy perfection. "Why don't you do this for the final? It's better than any restaurant food I've eaten."

"It'll take more than a bacon roll to win. The competition is tough."

"Win, eh? I thought you were all about the experience. Didn't you say taking part was all that mattered?"

"I did," Elijah said. "Now I'm all about winning. I want to destroy the competition."

Daniel laughed. Elijah had always been so laid back and easygoing. It was strange to see him with such a fire in his belly. "Who are they? The competition?"

"Keeley Rank and Joshua Shakeshaft."

Keeley Rank was a gossip columnist turned true life crime author. She was also a massive media whore with an opinion on anything that might grab her a headline, famed for her right-wing views and personal attacks on celebrities and politicians, which she carried out via public spats on social media. "How did Keeley make it to the final? I thought she'd be a terrible cook. She could sour milk with a poisoned tweet."

"She's one of the most competitive people I've ever met. And a fast learner. I doubt she went near a kitchen before coming on the show, but now she's there, she's doing everything she can to win."

"Is she as awful as she appears?"

Elijah shrugged. "Not really. I would say she gets a bad deal in the press but most of it is her own doing. She's one of those characters that people love to hate and she thrives on it. But from what I've seen of her, she's a pussycat."

"A pussycat who'll tear you to shreds?" Daniel asked, fixing himself another roll.

"Hell, yeah. She'd do me over in a heartbeat if there was a headline in it for her."

Daniel laughed. "Thought so. What about the other guy? Who is he again?"

"Joshua Shakeshaft."

"Shakeshaft? With a name like that I feel I *should* have heard of him, but I've got nothing."

"We're both *way* too old to have heard of him. He's an 'internet sensation'. Vlogging, blogging and all that stuff young people do."

"Right," Daniel said, rolling his eyes. "Then I definitely *haven't* heard of him."

"He's got millions of followers online and makes a fortune from advertisements and endorsements, so he's got a smart head on his shoulders. He's a nice kid. I like him."

"But you're still going to destroy him, right?"

"Bet your sweet sexy ass I am." Elijah laughed. "Take no prisoners—that's my motto now. That kid is going down." He mimed a two-finger gunshot.

* * * *

The day passed quickly.

They made love in the afternoon, taking their time on the living room floor, clinging to each other in a hot, slippery mess. Daniel didn't want it to end. He wrapped his arms and legs around Elijah, gripping him, wanting him deep, wanting it to last. When they were done, completely spent, he tried to keep him close.

But Elijah had to practice and kept returning to the kitchen.

Daniel spent time in the garden, enjoying the late-afternoon sun with a pile of Sunday papers and a chilled glass of chardonnay, his mobile switched off. Nothing would spoil the peace of today. Even the incessant buzz of neighboring lawn mowers kept a respectful distance.

"Dinner," Elijah called at last.

They usually ate their meals in the kitchen, but for this occasion Elijah had set the table in the dining room. He'd put out candles and napkins within silver rings.

"Wow," Daniel said, taking his seat. "You've really gone to town."

"Nothing but the best for you," he said, kissing him on the cheek before pouring them each a glass of champagne.

Elijah served the menu he'd chosen for the final task of *Top Cook*, when the remaining competitors would have two and a half hours to produce a three-course meal for the judges. To start he served crispy salmon fishcakes wrapped in smoked bacon with a homemade tartar sauce.

Daniel was fascinated by the advancements Elijah had made since he saw him last. His food already tasted great, but the real progress came with his presentation. The portion size and the arrangement on the plate were comparable with the best restaurants Daniel had eaten in.

"This is amazing," he said, savoring the complex flavor and textures of the dish.

Elijah looked hopefully across the table. "You're not just saying that because you're my boyfriend? I need to get this right. If anything is off, you have to tell me."

"It's exquisite. Honestly. Don't change a thing."

The second course surpassed the first. Roast venison fillet with apple puree and rosemary sauce, with celeriac mash and glazed carrots.

"I can't believe I'm eating this at home," Daniel remarked as he cut into the meat, which Elijah had cooked to perfection.

"I know how you hate having blood on your plate," Elijah said, "so I cooked this how you'd like it. But I'll serve it much rarer for the judges."

"Smart move." Daniel knew his preference for well-done meat was hopelessly out of step with most people's tastes. "Those guys will want it well under."

Elijah rounded off the meal with a dessert of chocolate raspberry pudding cake, with fresh raspberries and Greek yogurt. It was the perfect end to a perfect meal.

Afterward, Daniel took him to bed to give him his reward.

"You'll win for sure," he said, dropping to his knees at the foot of the bed to take Elijah's cock in his mouth.

"Oh, God." Elijah gasped, thrusting his fingers into Daniel's hair. "It doesn't really matter. I'm already a winner."

Daniel took his time, sucking gently and tugging at his balls in the way that drove him crazy. Each time he sensed Elijah come close to end, he relaxed his grip, prolonging the excruciating pleasure. He took him to the edge again and again until he knew Elijah couldn't stand it any longer. He came in Daniel's mouth in a wild, abundant rush.

"Your turn." Elijah murmured afterward, raising Daniel onto the bed.

"You've already given me enough." He laughed as Elijah hauled off his underpants, releasing his hard cock.

"I can never give you enough," he said, taking him in one mouthful.

They lay together afterward, face to face, arms around each other's waists. A quiet, melancholic mood had settled over them as they realized the weekend was almost over. Tomorrow they would go their separate ways again, Daniel to Blackpool, Elijah to Edinburgh.

"It's only a couple of nights this time," Elijah said, drawing his fingers along Daniel's hip bone. "It'll be over before you know it."

"I know," he said wistfully, but two whole nights seemed like a lifetime.

They would be together again soon. And this time nothing would keep them apart.

Chapter Four

The six-thirty-nine train from York didn't arrive at Edinburgh Waverley Station until nine-twenty. The producers of *Celebrity Top Cook* wanted Elijah on set for eight, but this was the earliest train. He would have had to travel up last night and miss out on precious time with Daniel. After two weeks apart, that wasn't an option.

"Start without me," he told them over the phone as the train sped north from Newcastle. "I'll make up the time."

He knew there wouldn't be anything to make up. The first challenge of the day wasn't due to start until ten at the Officers' Club. They were only called early to allow time for hair and makeup and to dress in their chef's whites, none of which would take more than a few seconds for Elijah. He would slip on the overalls and a chef's hat when he arrived and be good to go. The hotel was situated in the heart of the city and he could make it in a taxi from the station in under five minutes.

Elijah tried to use the time on the train to focus on the tasks ahead, but his mind kept wandering back to Daniel, still sleepy and warm in bed when he left the house earlier. Every time they separated, it ripped Elijah to the core — a visceral pain. This morning was no different. At least it wouldn't be long. Filming on *Top Cook* was due to wrap on Tuesday, followed by an after-show party for the crew. Elijah would be on the train to Blackpool first thing on Wednesday morning. Better than the two-week separation they'd just endured. Still, every hour was a torment.

Before Daniel, he'd needed no one. Not like this. He'd been in relationships, but nothing serious. Two years was the longest he'd ever lasted before. He'd had a boyfriend in college — all very casual. He'd once shared a flat in Birmingham with a production runner, more for convenience than any great desire for each other. When work took Elijah elsewhere, the relationship had fizzled out. There had been no tears on either side. It wasn't that important.

Other than that, there'd been a couple of boyfriends and a series of dates that went nowhere. He'd had an on-off thing with a comedian called Jack Joel for a while, but it was mostly off. Jack was hugely ambitious and insecure. His rivalry had ruined any real chance of romance. But Elijah had never been lonely. He hadn't been looking for love. He'd enjoyed his freedom , going where the work took him without a care for anyone other than himself.

Daniel had set a bomb under that independence and blown it sky high. It was his old life, one he didn't want anymore. All he wanted was Daniel, all the time.

The train arrived in Edinburgh. As Elijah gathered his bags, he noticed a woman in the opposite row staring at him. Her face lit up when she caught his attention. She was in her fifties, wearing a stack of ethnic jewelry and peered at him through huge, thick-lensed glasses.

"Can I have your autograph?" she asked earnestly.

"Sure." He grinned, grateful she'd waited until the end of the trip before asking. He wasn't used to being such a public figure and it still made him uneasy. Despite appearing on TV for many years, he'd been able to stroll around unnoticed for most of the time. That had all changed after his voyage on *The Atlantic Anthem* and the publicity it had garnered. Even now, he refused to accept that he'd done anything to earn his celebrity status, that he was only famous for being famous.

"What are doing in Edinburgh?" the woman asked.

"I'm here for *Celebrity Top Cook*," he said, handing her the autograph he had signed on the back of a menu card.

"Oh, I love that show. When is it on?"

"Not till the autumn." He smiled, hating to be rude, but he didn't have time for idle chat. "Nice to meet you. Enjoy the rest of your journey."

He snagged his case and hurried for the exit before the woman's interest in him attracted further attention.

Luckily, he caught a cab straight off the rank and made it to the Officers' Club for nine-thirty. The club and hotel were situated in an enormous townhouse on one of the city's arresting Georgian streets. The road outside was closed to traffic, allowing the production and camera trucks access to the building, while pavements were crowded with people from the crew.

As Elijah reached through the window to pay the taxi driver, a voice behind him said, "How nice of you to join us."

Short, blonde and expensively groomed, Keeley Rank stood on the curb smoking a cigarette. During her days as a journalist she'd gained the nickname 'The Dwarf with the Poisoned Pen.' Even now, she took great delight in living up to it. Dressed in her chef's whites with her sleek hair fastened up in an elegant chignon, Keeley had taken full advantage of the makeup trailer to sport smoky eyes and jammy-red lips. She looked ready for a night on the town rather than a hot day in the kitchen.

"Were you worried about me?" he asked, dragging his case toward her.

"No. I thought you might have lost your nerve. Couldn't take the heat and all that."

"Sorry, old girl, but I couldn't give you the satisfaction. You might win if I wasn't here to beat you."

Keeley's smile only reached the edges of her mouth, never her eyes. "I'm *going* to win."

"You're going to win second or third place. Congratulations on that."

She snickered. "Quite sure of yourself, aren't you?"

"I've been practicing," he taunted.

Keeley drew on her cigarette and exhaled a slow cloud of smoke into his face. "Practice isn't everything. Not against natural talent. You can't rehearse *that*."

Elijah laughed. A lot of people took offense at the things Keeley said to their faces, but he found her funny. There was a dark sense of humor at work beneath the prickly exterior and he liked her a lot. He'd even read one of her books when they'd first met. She'd played a pivotal role in the capture of a serial killer a few years before. The Durham Strangler had slaughtered several young men and had been about to murder the actor Dale Zachary and his lover when Keeley had intervened. She had written two best-selling books about the killings, though her version of events had been called into question by many of those close to the case. None the less, her book was a fast-paced, well-written read, though perhaps best taken with a pinch of salt.

"Are we still good to go for ten?" he asked.

Keeley nodded and lit another cigarette. "There's no rush. The 'boy wonder' only rolled out of bed five minutes ago."

"See you in there," Elijah said, hurrying into the foyer of the club.

The interior was remarkable with its old-world décor, lots of dark-wood paneling and military insignia. He'd have liked time to explore and take it all in. But not today. Maybe he should bring Daniel here sometime and get to know the place better. Just the two of them with no commitments. *Why not?*

At the reception desk, he spotted Pascal, a young production assistant, and headed over.

"Where do I get ready?" he asked.

"Upstairs," she answered. "The second door on the left at the top of the stairs. Your clothes and everything are already there. Then we need you back outside to film your arrival."

"Two minutes," he said, hastening for the stairs.

Despite the inconvenience of being away from home, there was a lot to enjoy on the set of a show like this. Especially the excitement. There was always a buzz about the locations, wherever they went to film.

He hurried to the dressing room and found rails of white uniforms and black trousers. Elijah threw his bags into the corner and stripped to his navy briefs. He sprayed his entire upper body with deodorant and dressed in the chef's outfits.

"What's up, man?"

Joshua Shakeshaft, the 'boy wonder' as Keeley had tagged him, ambled into the room drinking a can of Red Bull. For a boy of twenty, rumored to have his first million already in the bank, Joshua looked like an unkempt, bedraggled student. He wore a baggy pair of shorts, dirty Converse and a Rolling Stones T-shirt. His thick blond hair stuck up at crazed angles. He didn't look as if he'd had a shower, or even slept much, since Elijah had seen him on Saturday. Beneath the mess of hair and dark-ringed eyes, a good-looking boy strove to get out.

"Whoa," Elijah said. "Rough weekend?"

Joshua shrugged. "Tidy enough. Where've you been?"

"Home."

Joshua grimaced. "Why, man? That's so lame."

"That's because I'm a lame old man."

The lackadaisical attitude was wholly deceptive. Keeley had written Joshua off, but Elijah wouldn't be fooled. The kid had made a fortune and had millions of online followers. He hadn't achieved that by being stupid or lazy. Just like he'd checked out Keeley's books, he'd also watched several of Joshua's video blogs. Most of it went over Elijah's head, but Joshua had an easy, funny way in front of the camera. He'd been uploading episodes since he was fourteen and was a natural at it. Beneath that messy exterior lurked an uncommonly shrewd and clever young man.

Keeley and Joshua were strong opposition. The judges on the show were tough and didn't put people through to the next round because they liked them, or that they were popular. It all came down to their talent in the kitchen. And these two has masses of it. The competition in the earlier stages had been easy. Fifty percent of the celebrities taking part barely had the skills to boil an egg. The last couple of weeks had been tougher as the challenges increased in difficulty and the better cooks remained. Last week had saw the final five competitors reduced to three. Elijah had thought his time was up.

Amazingly, he'd made it through. Now he wanted to win. He liked Keeley and Joshua, but he intended to obliterate them and take the trophy himself.

* * * *

They sat in the back of a taxi with a cameraman as it drove around the block.

"Look pensive," the director told them.

The taxi pulled up in front of the hotel and Elijah, Keeley and Jake stepped out, looking up as if seeing the club for the first time and being overwhelmed by the gravitas of the moment, before heading up the steps to the entrance.

"Cut," yelled the director. "Let's do that one more time."

"Oh, for fuck's sake, why?" Keeley wailed. "Can't we get in the bloody kitchen and start cooking?"

"You had your head down in the taxi," the director informed her. "If you want us to use a shot of your double chin, then by all means skip the reshoot."

"I have not got a double chin," she said indignantly, spinning around and marching straight back to the taxi.

Elijah smiled and stayed quiet. The chances were they all had double chins on camera. Each of them had gained weight over the course of the show. He'd put on at least six pounds. As soon as this was over, he had to hit the gym.

After another two takes, driving around the block and arriving at the hotel, the director nodded, happy with the footage, and they moved on to the interiors.

Elijah, Keeley and Joshua assembled in the club dining room, once again looking pensive on cue while the presenters and judges of *Celebrity Top Cook* were filmed arriving to address them.

Pete Jericho, a rotund Yorkshire man, had judged the show since its inception. He'd found fame as a TV chef in the mid-1990s. At sixty years old, Pete was a bizarre sex symbol and pinup for viewers. He'd been married four times, with each of his wives younger and more beautiful than the one before.

His co-judge, Bruce Brooks, was another unlikely middle-aged heartthrob. Dubbed the 'thinking woman's crumpet', Bruce had first come to fame as a fresh-faced TV chef in the 1990s. Twenty years later, older and heavier, he tried to maintain that sexy image.

'He's had two hair transplants and never goes out in public without a control vest,' Keeley had informed Elijah early in the run. *'And he's a total player. He's had more women than hot dinners, and looking at the gut, you can see he's had a lot of dinners.'*

Despite the criticism they frequently came under, Pete and Bruce were icons of the show. Their personalities had been instrumental to its success. Without them, it would be just another cookery program, cluttering up the TV schedules.

"This is it," Pete announced loudly once the cameras were in position and filming. "There are only two challenges remaining until one of you is crowned the new *Celebrity Top Cook*."

Elijah couldn't stop grinning. He must look like a lunatic. How many times had he watched the show and heard those words said to other celebrities? *This is unreal.* A shiver of excitement went down his spine. He looked to his competitors, both of whom appeared intensely serious. *Lighten up*, he thought. Sure, he wanted to win as much as they did, but not at the expense of the experience. It was a big deal, being in the final three, and he was determined to enjoy it.

Bruce Brooks took up the next link. "This afternoon at one, you'll serve a three-course lunch to thirty members of the Great North Air Ambulance Service. That's one course each. You'll find a fully stocked larder in the kitchen. We want each of you to create one course from your chosen ingredients. Decide between you who is doing what. You have two and a half hours starting…now."

It was always the same. With the challenge revealed, Elijah's adrenaline kicked in.

They hastened to the kitchen, followed by the camera crew.

"I'll do the dessert," Keeley said firmly.

"Shouldn't we discuss it first?" Elijah asked.

"There's nothing to discuss. I'm doing the dessert."

He knew what she was up to. She wanted to cook the sweet, so she'd have longer to prepare. Whoever drew the starter would have the least time to get ready.

"Whatever," he said. Desserts were his weakest area. He was better suited to savory dishes. Still, time was tight.

"What do you want to do?" Joshua asked him.

"Let's check out the larder before we decide. Better see what we have to work with before making a judgment."

"I'm still doing the third course," Keeley snipped.

"You've got it," Elijah said, hoping she fucked it up magnificently.

As always, the larder was packed with an awesome selection of ingredients — meat, fish, vegetables, salads, fruits, as well a huge choice of canned and jarred products. Deciding what to cook was almost as difficult as pulling it off.

"I'd really like to do the main," Joshua said, eyeing up a great tray of fillet steaks.

"Fine." Elijah had already spotted a plate of fresh mackerel. The fish would make an excellent starter, light and tasty. He carried the plate to his counter. Going out first, there was no time to lose. He filleted the fish straight away — he'd think about how he would serve them as he went.

"Hang on," Keeley blurted. As she looked at the array of produce, he saw from her face that she didn't have a clue what to do. "I'm not sure about a dessert anymore."

"Tough. You called it, you've got it. We don't have time to talk about it."

"Don't be a twat. That's not fair. We need to discuss what we're all doing before we decide."

"You made your decision and you got what you wanted."

"Yeah," Joshua yelled. "I'm doing steak." He possessively covered the meat as he carried it to his own counter.

Keeley's eyes narrowed, though her botoxed brow remained astonishingly line-free. The camera crew, sensing drama, zipped in to catch the moment. "There's fuck all here to make a dessert with. You've stitched me up, you bastards."

"Language," the director shouted. "We can't have swearing on prime-time television."

"Oh, fuck off," Keeley barked. "Bleep the fucker out. How the hell am I expected to cook when there's nothing here? It's all savory shit."

"There's plenty of dessert ingredients," Elijah said. He saw chocolate, cream, eggs, fresh fruit, sugar, cream cheese. She had dozens of options to choose from.

"One of you can swap with me," she said fiercely.

"I'll do no such thing." He'd already gutted and filleted two fish in the time she'd been bitching.

"I'm doing steak," Joshua said. He could be very sure of himself when he had to be.

"Damn it." Keeley shoved random items onto a tray. Chocolate, apples, cheese. "And if you edit this to make me look like a cunt, I'll sue every one of you bastards."

Elijah chuckled. They'd have to edit her all right, just to cut out the swearing.

He'd decided what to do with his mackerel when Pete Jericho came along with a camera crew to ask him about it. "I will pan fry the fish till the skin is nice and crispy and serve that with a potato and beetroot salad and freshly made horseradish sauce."

"Nice." Pete smacked his lips. "And can you do all that in the time?"

"Absolutely." He raised his voice his make sure his next comment could be overheard. "And the best thing about going first is that I'll be able to sit back and relax while Keeley makes a mess of her dessert."

Her response came soaring back across the kitchen. "I'll make a mess of your arse if you don't keep your big mouth shut."

Elijah laughed, playing up to the camera. The competition might be tough, but he was having the time of his life.

Chapter Five

Daniel arrived back in Blackpool mid-afternoon. He didn't have to be at the theater for the evening show until six, but there seemed little point hanging around at home once Elijah left. It was a curious thing. He'd owned the house for years before meeting Elijah and had lived there happily on his own all that time. But it wasn't just his home anymore. It was *their* home. Without Elijah, he didn't feel the same about the place. He missed him too much. The empty rooms only stressed his absence, mocking him with their silence.

If he had to be alone, he'd rather be at the hotel.

The lead players in *Lady Lynda* were staying at The Majestic, a five-star hotel on the north shore of the resort. Daniel and Max LaFranchi had luxury suites for the duration of the run. Hotel living had never appealed much, but he might as well take advantage while it was there. *Better than going stir-crazy at home.*

Daniel's room on the sixth floor, just below Max, containing every convenience and comfort he could want. A massive bedroom with a king-sized bed. A large, separate living room with two leather sofas, art deco-style lamps and paintings in ornate frames. It also boasted a well-stocked bar with a separate champagne fridge. The champagne, he'd discovered, was on Max's rider, and the producers, assuming the leading man would want the same, had provided it. Daniel didn't object. When Elijah got here on Wednesday they would sink a bottle or two.

The best features of the room were the vast windows that offered splendid views of the Irish Sea. Despite those days on the *Anthem*, Daniel hadn't lost his love for the sea. Coming in late from a show, he liked to throw the windows wide and enjoy a nightcap, listening to the waves hitting the shore.

Being away from home did have some perks.

He unpacked the clean clothes he'd brought and returned to the living room. He opened the windows to let that fresh sea air into the suite and put on some music. A little light opera. Alfie Boe suited his mood.

It was too late for lunch in the restaurant so he called room service and requested a crayfish and rocket sandwich with lemon mayonnaise on Mediterranean bread. *Room service, another perk of hotel living*. He helped himself to a bottle of sparkling water from the bar while he waited for the food to arrive.

One day became much like another when he was working on a long show. He'd have lunch and rest a little, then hit the hotel gym for an hour around four-thirty, before heading to the theater. It seldom varied unless they had a matinee, in which case he skipped the gym. Two shows a day provided more than enough exercise.

Still, he didn't have long to go. The run was nearly over. Performers often grumbled about the comedown they experienced at the end of a show. He'd experienced it himself in the past but knew it wouldn't happen this time. Not with Elijah to combat the blues. There were plans to make, a holiday to book. If he could get to the end of the week, they could go wherever they wanted.

A sudden knock at the door cut short Daniel's introspection. It couldn't be room service, not already. Getting up, he opened the door on two familiar faces, Rachel Lopez and Alisha Cameron.

"Hi." Alisha beamed. "We weren't sure you were back. Can we come in? It won't take long."

"Sure."

The women followed him into the living room.

Alisha Cameron, along with her husband, theater impresario Marcus Cameron, was the producer of *Lady Lynda*. A striking woman in her late fifties, with coco skin and lush, copper-toned hair, she always dressed immaculately in couture suits and handmade shoes. An actress herself when she was younger, she had appeared in several successful TV and stage shows, before realizing she was happier behind the scenes.

Rachel Lopez, the director of *Lady Lynda*, was an immensely successful trans woman. Formerly known as Richard, she had once been a theatrical producer herself. Having fully transitioned in her mid-thirties, Rachel had become a director and had been at the top of her game for twenty years. She wore her shoulder-length blonde hair in a bob and would never be seen without a lashing of statement jewelry, mostly silver. Today, she showed off her long, toned legs in a black suit with a short skirt.

"How was your weekend?" Rachel asked, crossing to the bar and helping herself to a Diet Coke. "Did you find time for Elijah?"

"I did. Not nearly enough, but he's coming down here on Wednesday, so I'll see him."

"Good. It'll be nice to see him again."

"You make a terrific couple," Alisha enthused. "So handsome together."

"All right, ladies," Daniel said with good humor. "There's no need to butter me up. Whatever it is you're after, let's hear it."

"That's what I like about you," Rachel said. "No bullshit messing about. You get straight to the point. Like me."

Alisha moved to the sofa and perched, displaying her own incredible legs. Daniel sat opposite her. He had a lot of respect for these women. They treated every member of the team with the same degree of professionalism and were a pleasure to work for. But they took no prisoners and dealt with any bad behavior at the root. When one of the supporting actors had tried to smuggle an underaged fan into his dressing room early in the run, they'd swiftly replaced him.

Rachel sat beside Alisha.

"We need to talk about London," Alisha said.

He'd expected as much. They're been on at him about the West End transfer since the show had opened to rave reviews and full houses earlier in the summer.

"Look," he said, "I understand that you need to move forward, and your backers want to know the names you have involved before committing, but I've already explained that I need a break before pledging myself to a big run. This has been my first job since I was injured. It's been great. I've loved every minute, but I don't know if I'm ready for the pressure of a London run. I hope you understand that."

"We do. Absolutely," Alisha said.

"But hear us out," Rachel said. "Circumstances have shifted somewhat, and I think you might like what we've got to offer."

"As you know, we originally planned to take the show to London for Christmas," Alisha continued. "Which, I guess, was one of the problems you had. You'd have a few weeks off but would be back into rehearsal by October. Well, the theater we wanted has fallen through so we're not in a position to open this side of Christmas."

"Okay," Daniel said thoughtfully. They were right. The prospect of leaving Blackpool and going straight into preproduction on another run didn't thrill him. He wanted some time off. A holiday. A year ago, he could have gone from one job to another without a day in between. After the *Anthem*, things were different. He had to recharge his batteries, mentally if not physically. "I'm listening."

"The London run won't happen until March," Rachel said. "We don't have to start rehearsals until late January. That gives you the rest of this year to do whatever you want."

"And that's not even the best part." Alisha beamed. "Get this—we've only gone and booked the London Palladium. Can you believe that? The goddamn Palladium."

"Wow," he said. The Palladium, perhaps the most famous theater in London, if not the whole of the UK. The place where all performers, no matter how big, aspired to perform. He'd been on the stage before, as part of a variety show, but never in a full-time engagement.

"We don't want your answer today," Alisha said, "but promise us you'll think about it. Okay? We'd like to put out a press release before the final show on Saturday. It would be great if we could say the entire cast of this hit production will transfer to the Palladium next year."

"It won't be the same without you," Rachel added.

"I don't know what to say." The news was exciting. It was something he'd always wanted — that stage, that audience — and yet, could he do it? Did he have what it took to get up there? He used to, no doubt about it. *But now?*

"Just say you'll think about it," Alisha said.

"That's all we need from you today," Rachel asserted.

"Yes," he said, still trying to get his head around the proposition. "I'll definitely think about it."

* * * *

"Hold on, I've got a message for you." The stage door attendant stopped Daniel as he arrived at the theater. "Two guys dropped by earlier. They said they knew you. Said they were friends of yours."

"Thanks," Daniel said, taking the folded piece of paper and hurrying down the corridor. He was running late. There'd been an accident on the promenade and his driver had had to take him on a circuitous route through the back streets of town to reach the theater. He had less than half an hour to get ready for curtain-up.

He was word perfect and knew every beat of the show by heart, but hated to be late. His obsessive punctuality wouldn't quit.

Reaching his dressing room, he threw the message on top of the table and stripped quickly. His clothes for the opening number were already on the hanger. He'd showered before leaving the hotel so he gave himself a fresh squirt of deodorant and put on the costume.

Joe, his dresser arrived, as he buttoned up his shirt. "Cutting it a little fine, aren't you?"

"Too fine for my liking," he said, sitting down so Joe could fix the head mic and conceal the wires beneath his hair.

Joe was unrufflable. Stress was not a word in his vocabulary. He took his time with the mic, brushing Daniel's hair into place with the tips of his fingers. His own hair had been styled into a fastidious coif. Daniel studied it in the mirror and wondered how long it took Joe to get ready. His clothes were casual but worn for effect. The top buttons of his crew neck jersey were undone to offer a flash of his lightly tan chest and his chino shorts were turned up above the knee to show off his downy blond calves.

"How was the romantic weekend?" Joe asked.

"Over too soon," Daniel answered.

"And how's the lovely Elijah? Is he missing us all here in Blackpool?"

"He's very well and looking forward to seeing everyone this weekend." Daniel concealed a smile. Joe tried to act cool and nonchalant, but everyone knew what a massive crush he had on Elijah. Whenever Elijah visited the theater, Joe mooned after him with enormous, dilated pupils, like an overexcited kitten.

As Joe ran the connectors down his shirt to the power pack sewn into his trousers, Daniel finally picked up the note that had been left at the door. He received a lot of messages via the theater. Fan mail, requests for autographs, well wishes and such. He usually set aside one afternoon a week to answer it, replying to all his own fan mail. There could sometimes be a backlog, especially after a TV performance or record release, but he always got around to answering.

This was different, just a quick note.

"Oh, my God," he said, reading the message.

"Something nice or sometime awful?" Joe asked. "Or something filthy you can't tell me about?"

Daniel laughed. "I doubt there's anything that could shock you."

"You'd be right. Some of the things I've seen back here, I could write a book, but no one would believe me."

"This won't make your book, but it's pretty great all the same," he said, scanning the note again. "Two old friends I haven't seen in a long, long time. They're in the house tonight."

Hi Daniel,
Christian and I are in for the show. Be great to see you later if you can spare the time. Ben.

There was a phone number written in a careful hand at the bottom of the page.

Ben Delaney and Christian Gates—Daniel couldn't remember when he'd last seen either of them. It had to be ten years or more.

"Who are they? Old cast mates?"

"No. We were in a band together. The first proper job I ever had. A boy band called Overload. We were only kids."

Joe's olive-green eyes watched him carefully in the mirror. "Overload? Isn't that the group you were in with…?"

"Oliver Gill," he said calmly.

"The guy who tried to kill you?"

"Oliver was there before my time. We were never in the band together. But yes, that was Overload."

"What are these guys like? Not like *him*, I hope."

"Nothing at all," Daniel said. "They kicked him out because of his bad attitude and behaviour. That's how I got the break in the first place, as Oliver's replacement. I can't believe they're here."

Like so many old friends, he felt a sense of guilt that they'd drifted apart. When the band had broken up, they'd made promises to stay in touch, to always be friends. The kind of youthful ideas that are hard to follow through. Their careers and lives had taken them in different directions. They weren't even Facebook friends. *How feeble is that?*

Joe tapped his shoulder. "You'll all done." He took a step back and removed Daniel's jacket from the hanger, gesturing for him to stand. "I hope they're not jealous of you. Not like that other bastard. I'm sorry to speak ill of the dead, but nobody needs friends like that."

"Don't worry on that score. Ben and Christian were great guys. The very best. I was the youngest in the band, and they always had my back."

"People can change."

"Not these two."

"I hope you're right."

"I am," he said and felt sure of it. The hostilities around Overload had died with Oliver.

There was nothing left to fear.

Chapter Six

Elijah wanted nothing more than a hot bath and a comfortable bed. It had been a long day with the early train from Leeds and a full eight hours of cooking on the show. Following the challenge at the Officers' Club, the crew had taken him aside to film various insert pieces to camera. There would be no actual winner from today's task. The judges were watching and making notes for their ultimate selection tomorrow. Even so, he knew he'd done well. His mackerel dish received the most favorable comments from the lunchtime diners and despite being pushed for time, he'd achieved everything he wanted with the dish.

Joshua had also had a decent round. He ran out of time and had to omit one of the side dishes from his main course, but what he served went down well.

Keeley hadn't been so lucky. Her dessert was a catastrophe. She attempted to tackle a fruit tart with custard. The pastry of her tart was undercooked and soggy while the custard came out a curdled mess. She swore her head off throughout the challenge and had to be admonished by the director when she threw a pan of boiled milk at a cameraman. Luckily, she was a lousy shot and missed her intended target.

Elijah hadn't ruled her out of the competition, and as they headed into the final day, she ranked third of the three of them. But she was a fighter. She would use every tool in her armory to win tomorrow.

He wouldn't let that happen.

The title belonged to him. It was so close he could almost touch it.

An early night and plenty of rest was in order. But first, a drink.

The entire crew were staying at a hotel called The McDonald on Edinburgh's Royal Mile. Tomorrow's final round would be filmed in the kitchens here. Like so many of the hotels in the city, it was a beautiful old building, ingrained with history. Many of the original features were retained — granite floors, sandstone walls and open fireplaces. There were modern twists to the decor with gold and red carpets, comfortable sofas and lush throws, but each piece kept in perfect harmony with the old-world style.

Elijah passed through the foyer, taking in the grand staircase with its stone balustrades. He loved this place, so much character and history. He vowed to come back to Edinburgh soon, with Daniel. They could take their time, exploring the city, maybe stay a whole week. The streets, the castle, the old vaults beneath South Bridge — said to be haunted by an evil entity — the bars, the restaurants, the parks. Daniel would love it.

The main bar was relatively quiet when he entered. Most of the crew were in the restaurant for dinner. He resolved to have one drink before retiring to his room to prepare for tomorrow. With a large wrap party planned for the following evening, he would mix with the crew then. Tonight, he wanted to be alone.

A young man stood behind the bar. He didn't look much over eighteen, slight and attractive in an atypical way. He had his own look. Cute and kind of sexy.

"Hello," he said. "What can I get for you?"

Elijah couldn't place his accent. It certainly wasn't Scottish. More Eastern European. Polish, perhaps.

What time is it? Gone nine. Later than he thought. "Could I get a vodka martini?" he asked.

The waiter nodded. "Sir. How would you like that?"

"With three olives."

"A dirty martini," said a voice from behind him. "Exactly how I like it. Make that two and bring them over. We'll take that table in the window."

Keeley. She had freshened up after her afternoon in the kitchen and wore a long red top with black pants. She'd washed and restyled her hair and had reapplied her full makeup.

"Don't think you can trick me into getting drunk," Elijah said with good humor as he followed her to the window seats. "I'm having one drink then going to bed."

"That's the difference between us," Keeley said, sitting down. "Such an underhand tactic hadn't even occurred to me."

"I'll bet it hadn't."

"Don't make any bets about tomorrow unless your money is all on me. Or you can afford to lose big."

He laughed. She had balls, he'd give her that. Despite what he'd thought earlier, the competition remained wide open. Keeley had sustained a hit today. It didn't mean he could write her off.

"How's your room?" he asked.

"Creepy." She shuddered. "I'll need a bucket of martini just to sleep in there tonight. I hate these old places. Give me a new-build airport Hilton any day."

"I think it's magnificent. All this history and atmosphere."

"It's old and depressing, that's what it is. I can hardly breathe. The atmosphere is so oppressive."

"Rubbish."

"When you wake up in the middle of the night and find a headless spirit sitting on the end of your bed, don't come crying to me."

"I'm not afraid of ghosts," he said. "It's the living who hurt you, not the dead."

"You don't have to convince *me* of that."

Their drinks arrived. Keeley watched the waiter with sharp eyes. His hands trembled, but he set them down without spilling a drop.

"He's frightened of you." Elijah chuckled as the boy left.

"Good. That's exactly how I like men. Afraid of me."

"You don't scare me," he said, tasting his martini. It was perfect.

"Give me time," she said expansively, sipping her own drink. She pursed her lips, seeming to approve.

She was some lady. Elijah hadn't met anyone like her. She had a fearsome reputation and was loathed by certain sections of the media. She'd once appeared on a lighthearted current affairs program. Keeley had been making headlines at the time for a damning article she'd written about working mothers and their rights to childcare — they had none, in her opinion. The other participants on the program had gone to town, tearing her to shreds. It was typical of her brand of journalism.

To provoke and stir it up. She liked to piss people off, saying things to get them rattled.

Elijah saw through it. Keeley Rank wasn't all that bad.

"This place reminds me of Durham," she said. "Ever been?"

"Briefly," he said. "I did a comedy gig there once, but it was an in and out thing. I didn't stay more than a few hours."

"I know it well. Too well. From when I caught The Durham Strangler. It's a lot smaller than Edinburgh but the same in a lot of ways. All these old buildings and history. Too much history, if you ask me. It bogs you down."

Elijah fished one of the olives out of his drink and crushed it between his teeth. It was booze-soaked and salty. Delicious. "I've been reading your book," he said. "About the strangler. Scary guy."

"He was an insecure, inadequate piece of shit," she said, taking another drink. "Most killers are. They take their failures out on the rest of the world. But you know that better than I do. Oliver Gill—now he was one majorly fucked-up, pathetic inadequate. He might as well have worn a sign saying 'killer'."

Elijah stiffened and knocked back his drink. He had realized too late and walked right into her trap. "I don't like to talk about Oliver."

"You should. If you keep your emotions locked up, they can turn toxic on you."

"I'm not bottling anything up," he insisted. "What happened is history. Over and done with. It won't do any good to go over it again."

Keeley leaned forward. Her eyes were bright. "Let me be the judge of that. If you told your story to me, I could secure a book deal tomorrow. There's already an offer on the table but I know I can better it. Publishers will cut each other's throats for this book."

So that was her game. Everybody had an angle and this was hers. "Sorry, Keeley. I've heard every offer before and I'm not interested. *We're* not interested."

"I'm not talking about some shitty, ghost-written account," she announced eagerly. "This will be your story—yours and Daniel's—as told to me. Whatever offer you've had you can double it and add a zero to the end of it. The story is too hot not to be told."

He shoved out his chair and stood. "It won't be told by me or Daniel. So let's just leave it at that. Now, excuse me. I'm going for an early night so I can whoop your arse tomorrow."

"I will write the book," she called behind him. *"Whether you cooperate or not."*

Elijah dug his fingernails into his palms. *Keep it together.* He was fuming inside, but he'd be damned if he let her see it.

The past kept coming back to haunt them. *Will we ever be able to put Oliver-fucking-Gill behind us?*

* * * *

"Shit, man. It's so good to see you."

Daniel wrapped his arms around Ben Delaney and hugged him tight.

"You were fantastic tonight," Ben said, squeezing him back. "The baby of the band is all grown up."

"None of us are babies anymore." Daniel laughed. "You look fantastic. You both do."

He turned to take Christian Gates in an equally strong embrace.

It was the first time he'd seen them in fourteen years and time seemed to fall away, as if they'd never been apart.

Ben and Christian had come to his dressing room after the show. He'd recognized them as soon as they opened the door. They were older, more mature, and yet they also looked exactly the same.

Ben Delaney had always been a good-looking boy. With skin the shade of milk chocolate, he had the warmest, dark brown eyes. At six foot two, he was the tallest member of Overload, but in the years since then he'd grown into his statuesque frame. Tall, broad and muscular, he was in exceptional shape. He wore his black hair cropped close to his head and sported a short, neatly trimmed beard. Despite all that, his smile had always been his greatest feature. Wide and white, it had lost none of its power. As he grinned at Daniel, it was infectious.

Christian Gates had aged just as well. Originally from Norway, he had the blue-eyed, blond good looks that his Scandinavian heritage would suggest. He showed the slightest hint of gray in the hair around his temples and a few faint lines around his eyes, but otherwise he looked exactly how Daniel remembered. Tight, trim and beautiful.

Both guys looked better now than when they'd been pitched as teen heartthrobs.

"Come in," Daniel said. "Let's have a drink to celebrate."

After reading Ben's note, he'd arranged for a bottle of chilled champagne to be waiting after the show.

"Congratulations," Christian said, drifting around the room, taking in the cards and gifts from well-wishers and fans. "I always knew you'd make it big someday. You deserve it. You were wasted in Overload."

"I think we all were." Ben laughed. "God, as a boy band, we were so lame. What were we thinking?"

"We were just kids," Daniel said, handing them each a glass. "We didn't know what we were doing, we just did what we were told."

"*Stand here, move there, smile, smile, smile,*" Ben said. "I cringe every time I think about those days. Someone showed me some of our old stuff on YouTube recently. I couldn't believe how bad we were."

"It wasn't *all* bad," Daniel said, raising his glass. "We're here now, aren't we? Cheers."

"*Cheers.*"

They all clinked glasses.

Daniel stepped back to look at them again. How surreal, seeing them after all this time. He had nothing but good memories of Ben and Christian. The group had come to a premature end when they were dropped by their management and record label, but the boys themselves never had fallen out with each other. They'd talked about staying together, trying to secure another record deal, but the plans had come to nothing. Reality had intervened and they'd drifted in separate directions, trying to find work.

"So, what are you guys doing? How long are you here for?"

"We're staying at The Imperial," Christian said. "Just two nights. We came to see your show. Got no plans beyond that."

"You should have called ahead," Daniel said, "I could have met you this afternoon, or gone for dinner before the show."

"We didn't want to bother you," Ben said.

"It wouldn't be a bother," Daniel said. "C'mon, guys, you know me better than that. I hope you'll come back to the hotel with me. The Imperial is less than a mile from where I'm staying. I really want to catch up with what you're doing."

"You're on," Christian said.

"Love to." Ben flashed that dynamite smile.

Daniel stepped forward to top up their glasses. His emotions were all over the place, a confusion of happiness, nostalgia, affection, guilt and sadness. For a flopped pop band and a job that had lasted little more than a year when he was a teenager, he carried a lot of emotional baggage from Overload. His hand, holding the champagne, trembled.

Christian put a hand on top of his and squeezed gently. "I'm sorry. We should have got in touch sooner. After that thing with Oliver… I wasn't sure you'd want to hear from us again. Any of us. My biggest fear is that we'd reopen old wounds. I hope we haven't done that, turning up like this."

Daniel swallowed. "Of course not. No. I'm happy to see you. I really am."

Christian put an arm around him. "Good. I'm happy too."

Daniel allowed Christian to hold him for a moment. Christian had always had the knack of comforting and reassuring him. Daniel had lost his virginity to Christian, a long time ago, when the band was on a tour of Japan. There was no friction between them now. Passion had played a tiny part in what they'd done, even then. Daniel didn't love Christian, not in any sexual way—he had just been the right boy to experiment with. Christian was caring and safe. Daniel wouldn't have wanted it any other way.

"What happened with Oliver, man, that wasn't your fault," Ben said. "It was all his own doing. He was always unhinged. Know what he said to me the first time I met him?"

Daniel shook his head, taking a step back from Christian.

"He looked me up and down," Ben continued, "and he said, 'You must be our token black guy. I didn't know we were going down that route.'"

"What?"

"You never told me that," Christian said.

"I told nobody," Ben said with a grim laugh. "Token black guy. That's what he thought of me. He was a complete sociopath."

"Psychopath, more like," Christian said.

"He was a cunt," Ben added. "Nothing but trouble. You were unlucky, Daniel, that's all, running into him on that ship. Just the wrong place at the wrong time. He'd have done the same to any one of us, given a chance. He thought the entire world was his enemy. He always did."

"You're probably right," Daniel said.

"I am right. And that's as much as I want to talk about the bastard. We're here, he's not. Now let's get drunk. Let's show this town what happens to boy bands when we get old."

Chapter Seven

Time has been kind to Ben and Christian, Daniel thought as they chose a table in the near empty hotel bar. Sam LeFerve, the music manager who had put them together as a teenaged group, had an eye for potential talent. But even Sam could not have predicted what handsome men those fresh-faced boys would grow up to be.

He wondered about the rest of the group. There were five of them in Overload. Daniel, Ben, Christian, Luke Torrens and David Kharsa. He didn't even know where the other guys were, let alone what they looked like now.

It was inexcusable that he'd allowed their friendship to lapse. Fourteen years was a long time and they'd been so tight back then. It was laxity. Pure and simple.

"Tell me what you've been up to," Daniel said. "I want to hear it all."

"There's not much to tell," Ben replied. "You're the only one who remained in the public eye."

"Being in the public eye isn't everything. C'mon, what have you've been doing? Where do you live? Do you have family? Tell me."

A waitress arrived to take their orders. Ben ordered a beer, Christian a single malt and Daniel a glass of red wine.

"Christian can go first," Ben said. "He has more to tell."

Christian smiled, wide and attractive. It brought back all kinds of memories for Daniel. Of when they were young and innocent. The night Christian took his virginity in Japan, he had felt unstoppable. They'd had their whole lives ahead of them, knowing nothing about disappointment, stress or heartbreak. Getting fucked for the first time was just another adventure.

"All right," Christian began, putting both hands on the table. "I live in South London with my husband, Lars. When the group broke up, I went home to Norway for a while. That's where we met. When Lars got a job in London, I came with him and we were married there."

"How long ago?"

"Seven years. We've got two kids. Holly is five and Tom is four."

Daniel's eyes widened. "Children. Wow, that's amazing."

"Weird, huh?" Christian said. "Your old boyfriend is married with two kids?"

"If I was asked to predict what you'd be doing now, that wouldn't be it," Daniel admitted.

Christian pulled out his phone and tapped through a couple of screens before showing Daniel a picture of two young kids. They had the same blond hair and happy expressions as they posed in a garden with a small dog.

"They didn't have the best start in life," Christian continued. "Tom was removed from his mother at birth. Holly had already been taken into care by then. Thank God social services kept them together and didn't separate them. Their mother was a drug addict. She took heroin throughout her pregnancy. Tom was seriously ill when he was born, addicted to the shit himself."

"God, that's awful," Daniel said, looking again the photo of the smiling children.

"He's doing well now. He's a little slow in his learning but he's getting there. He just needs love and support."

"I'm sure he gets it. My God, Christian, what you've done is amazing. Being a father to two kids. Whose idea was it?" Daniel asked. "To put yourself forward for adoption?"

"We decided together. But Lars is a researcher for a TV company. He did a feature on children stuck in the care system and who need loving parents. It was heartbreaking, truly. We'd always talked about having kids, but that show was the catalyst we needed to do something about it."

"I'd love to meet them. You should have brought the whole family to see that show. They'd love it."

"Next time," he said. "It was a big enough deal coming to see you after all this time without the added complication."

The waitress brought their drinks to the table. Daniel watched Christian as she set them down. His words had struck a chord. Why should their reunion be a big deal? A moment like this should be celebrated. He realized it was his fault as much as anyone's. He could have reached out to the boys any time he wanted. He hadn't.

"You didn't say what you do now? Lars is a researcher, what about you?"

"Personal trainer," Christian said. "I hope to open my own gym in the next two years but for now, it's private client work. It's convenient, getting to choose what hours I work. I do the school runs and all that stuff."

"It explains why you look so good."

"And I don't?" Ben said in mock offense.

"You're doing all right," Daniel said, nudging his shoulder. "So c'mon, what's your story? What have you been up to?"

Ben grinned and two great dimples cut into his cheeks. Daniel had forgotten about those. The dimples were his thing. Back in the day, their teenage fans had gone crazy for them.

"Nothing as exciting as Christian."

"Are you single?"

"Yup. Divorced. Happily so. My ex was a total bitch. I was crazy for her, but she was just crazy. Like, totally mental. It's not all bad. I do have a beautiful daughter, Rachel, who's seven. She lives with her mother but is nothing like her. She comes to me every other week."

"This is surreal. I can't believe you're both daddies. It's so grown up."

They all laughed.

"It doesn't feel that way," Ben said. "I still feel like a kid. The same kid who sang on those awful songs."

"Me too," Christian agreed.

"So what do you do, Ben?"

"I'm a songwriter these days."

"He's selling himself short," Christian added. "He's a *successful* songwriter."

"I do okay."

"Anything I'd have heard?"

Ben listed off a reel of artists and groups he'd written for. They were all current acts. Reality show winners, a hot new boy band and an international pop diva. So current, he didn't know who some of them were.

"Bloody hell." Daniel laughed. "You *are* doing all right."

"You know, I believe Overload would still be around today if we'd been allowed to write our own songs. Think about it. All the manufactured boy bands who've had any kind of longevity wrote their own material in the end."

"I don't think we were put together with any thought for longevity," Christian said. "We were there to make a fast buck. Heavily processed with no room for maneuver, that was us."

"You're right," Daniel said, "but I was too young to know any different. I was just happy to be in a band. I didn't think about writing. I had nothing to write about."

"There's another reason why we weren't allowed a sliver of control after you joined us," Christian remarked.

The others looked at him, eyebrows raised.

"Oliver," he said at last.

Daniel nodded. He could believe it. He knew all about Oliver Gill and his disruptive behavior. By the time Daniel had replaced him, Oliver's conduct had become legendary. He'd argued constantly with the other guys. He'd fought with record producers, stylists and directors, demanding a bigger role, believing he was the lead and should be front and center. The other boys had come to hate him. Oliver hadn't cared. They were beneath him, barely worth his contempt. He was the star of Overload. The others were his backing singers.

"After he got rid of Oliver, Sam had to keep the rest of us in our place," Christian said. "That's why we did what were told, so he could keep control. Sam would never have allowed us to write our own songs. It would have given us too much freedom."

They finished their drinks and Ben signaled the waitress for another round.

"Sorry," Christian said.

"What for?" Daniel asked.

"Bringing Oliver up. The subject was supposed to be off limits."

"I don't mind," Daniel said at last. "He killed a girl, poisoned another dancer and stabbed me. I can't pretend it didn't happen."

"Crazy bastard." Ben sneered.

"Did either of you see him again?" Daniel asked. "After he left the band?"

Christian shook his head.

"I saw him," Ben said. "Once. Not to speak to, or anything like that. Shit, like I ever would. I'd cross the road to avoid the twat. But I was in Manchester for work. I don't know, maybe four years ago. I was in a bar when this cabaret act came on and it was him — Oliver."

"What was he like?"

"Lousy. Third rate by any standard. No one paid him much attention, just continued their conversations and ignored what happened on stage. He did the usual set of covers that you hear all the time. Michael Bublé, Bruno Mars. Not very well at that."

"Didn't you want to speak to him?" Daniel asked.

Ben twisted his face. "Never. I had my fill of him when I was eighteen. I didn't want to see him again, never mind speak."

* * * *

Max LaFranchi shared a car back to the hotel with Carmen John, a beautiful young actress from the ensemble of *Lady Lynda*. Carmen was bursting with excitement, having landed a lead role in *Chicago the Musical*. Carmen was to play Velma Kelly in a major UK tour of the show. With her endlessly long legs and stunning figure, she was perfectly cast. Max had played the rival part of Roxy Hart earlier in her career and had a great deal of affection for the show.

"This calls for a celebration," Max said.

"I haven't told the producers yet," Carmen said. "It means I won't be available for the London run of *Lynda*."

"This is your big break. They'll understand. You have to do what's right for your career."

"I'm kind of nervous. I've never had such a big part. And the tour runs for nine months with the possibility of extending if it does well."

"How old are you now?" Max asked.

"Twenty-five."

"Then you're ready for this. Trust me. You're at the perfect age to progress your career to the next level. Embrace it, darling."

Carmen giggled nervously. "You're right."

"I always am," Max said with a laugh. "Now come with me. One drink, I insist."

She took Carmen by the arm and led her from the car to the hotel. The bar would still be open for residents. One quick drink and they'd be off to bed and save the celebrations for later in the week. Max would arrange drinks and food one night after the show. The girl deserved it, landing such a big gig.

Max was surprised to enter the bar and find Daniel with a couple of strangers. *Very good-looking strangers.*

"Hello, handsome. What are you doing up so late?" she asked.

"Catching up with old friends," Daniel said, introducing Ben and Christian. "Come and join us."

Ben, a beautiful-looking man, stood and pulled up two chairs.

"Great show tonight," he said.

"You were there?" she asked, taking a seat right next to him. *God, he's sexy*, she thought, studying him closely. The strong jaw, richly colored skin, those dimples. *How old is he? Late twenties? Thirty?* Much too young for her. Still, no harm in looking. She might be old, but she wasn't blind.

"We were in the center of the stalls," he said. "Had probably the best view in the house. I'm not really into musicals, not like Daniel and Christian, but I thought it was awesome."

Carmen chatted to the other boys, and Max found herself with Ben's full attention. *Why not? What harm can there be in chatting to a cute guy?*

The waitress came across for their order.

"What will you have?" Ben asked.

"What are you drinking?" Max asked him.

"Beer," he replied. "But I was about to switch to Jack Daniel's."

"Sounds good," she said. "I'll have the same. Make them doubles."

Carmen asked for white wine.

"How do you know Daniel?" she asked.

"We were in a group together," Ben said.

"Overload?"

"The same."

Now Max really felt old. She couldn't remember Overload from their brief time in the spotlight, but after working with Daniel, she'd looked up their videos on YouTube. *They were boys. Fourteen years ago. How old was I then? Forty? Holy shit.*

She remembered a cute black kid from the videos. That had to be Ben.

My, he has grown up.

"So what prompted your visit? Are you planning a reunion?"

Ben laughed. Max leaned even closer to him. That smile, those dimples — he was dynamite.

"I don't think anyone is waiting for Overload to reform," he said. "Least of all us. No, we came to see Daniel. It's kind of a surprise. He didn't know we were coming."

Max looked at Daniel, who was deep in conversation with Carmen and the other boy. If their visit was a surprise, he seemed to appreciate it. The whole Oliver Gill business was still very raw. She wasn't sure how well he'd take to more people from that period in his life, but it didn't seem to faze him. Daniel was stronger and braver than he gave himself credit for. He'd realize it soon enough. Until then, Max felt protective toward him.

Maternal.

Which was not a word she'd use to describe the emotions Ben aroused in her.

No, they were much more indecent.

Her cheeks grew hot and her heart beat faster. There was a tension in her core — thrilling, exciting and a little scary. She couldn't remember the last man to bring about that kind of reaction.

The waitress returned with their drinks. Max took hers and swallowed appreciatively.

"So where are you from, Ben?"

"Birmingham, originally. But I've lived all over the place. Brighton, London, Manchester, wherever the work takes me. I'm a bit of a nomad that way."

"I know what you mean," she said. "I've spent two-thirds of my life living out of suitcases. Going from one hotel to the next."

"It must be in your blood."

"You've got that much right. I go a stir-crazy if I stay still for too long." She took another swallow of bourbon. The glass was almost empty. What the hell was she so nervous about? *Get a grip, girl. You'd think you'd never met a good-looking guy before.* On reflection, she realized that most of the great-looking men she'd met were gay. Guys like Daniel, unbelievably handsome but sadly unavailable. It was a cliché. *She* was a cliché. *Gay icon and fag hag.* "Say, are you straight?"

Oh my God. Max, shut up. What was she thinking? The damn question came out of her mouth unchecked. Max felt the heat as her face turned a furious shade of crimson.

Ben widened his beautiful brown eyes and broke into a wide, cheeky grin. "I am, Miss LaFranchi. Are you?"

"Oh, I'm so sorry. I don't know what came over me. I'm mortified."

Ben chuckled. "Don't worry about it." He moved his head closer to hers and spoke softly. "And in case you're interested…I'm single too."

He looked deep into her eyes, making his full intention known.

Max was flattered, flustered, confused — that Ben should be interested in her. And quite obvious about it. This was the last thing she'd expected when she'd come into the bar looking for a quiet drink. That a man as young as Ben, as perfect as Ben, would flirt with her. But it was nice he did. *Yes, nice. Why not?* A little attention hurt no one. She was older than he, but was hardly collecting her pension. What harm could it do to flirt?

"Let's have another drink," she said.

* * * *

Daniel came out of the bathroom, unsteady on his feet. He'd drunk more than he'd intended, especially for a work night. But it was good. He hadn't let his hair down like this in a long time. Not since he'd started rehearsing the show. He'd been focused on work, on his performance, that whole time. Even when he went out with Max and the crew, he'd never let down his guard. But with Ben and Christian, it surprised him how soon they'd fallen back into their old comfortable ways.

His memories of Overload were clouded by Oliver. Tonight, with these guys, he realized that the experiences hadn't all been bad. They'd had some terrific times together.

Returning to the bar, he found Christian alone at their table.

"Where did everybody go?" Daniel asked, slumping into the seat beside him.

"Didn't you notice the romance brewing across the table?" Christian asked.

"What? Ben and Carmen?"

Christian didn't miss a beat. "Clearly you didn't. No, Carmen went to bed alone. Ben and Max."

"What? No way, you're crazy."

"They were all over each other from the moment she sat down," Christian said. "They disappeared right after you went to the toilet. I don't think we'll see either of them again tonight."

Daniel burst out laughing. "Holy shit. I don't believe it."

"Believe me, it's true."

"I must be drunker than I thought. I didn't notice anything."

"Ben always had a thing for MILFs," Christian remarked.

True. Daniel remembered when they were young. While he went through his experimental phase with Christian and the other boys had been secretly screwing their teenage fans, Ben had always been more interested in the hair dressers and makeup assistants who groomed them for TV and photo shoots. He'd chased women in their thirties and older when he was still a teenager.

"So, some things never change," Daniel said.

"We did," Christian said.

"We were never more than buddies though, were we?"

"I guess not. Do you ever regret it?"

"What?"

"Having me for your first time? Not waiting until you found that special guy?"

Daniel shook his head. "I was sixteen and horny. There's no way I could have waited. I didn't find that special guy until I met Elijah. Imagine how frustrated I'd have been if I'd waited till nearly thirty to pop my cherry!"

They both laughed. There was no tension between them. No jealousy, no bad history. They'd had their moment a long time ago. They were different men at different stages in their lives. There was nothing left for either of them except friendship.

It was a great place to be.

"I'm beat," Christian said. "I'm gonna head back to the hotel. I can't see any point in waiting for Ben. I could be here all night."

"I'll ask the receptionist to call you a taxi," Daniel said, getting to his feet, succumbing to tiredness himself. *Time for bed.*

"No, it's not far," Christian said. "The walk will do me good. The fresh sea air helps me sleep."

"Okay." Daniel walked him to the door. "Listen, I have an engagement with Max tomorrow. It's a local charity gig. Won't take more than a couple of hours. Why don't we get together for a late lunch once we're done? I don't have to be at the theatre till evening."

"Sounds great. Text me the details in the morning."

They hugged their goodbyes in the foyer.

"Thank you for coming," Daniel said, holding on to him for just a moment longer. "It is good to see you."

"You too," Christian said, squeezing him back. "Now we've reconnected, there's no reason to lose touch again."

"No," Daniel said. "That's definitely not going to happen. I've got my friends back. I intend to keep them."

* * * *

It had gone three when Christian left The Majestic. A salty freshness came in from the sea. Christian breathed in deep, filling his lungs, invigorated. He set off toward the seafront, deciding to take the long route back to his hotel. He had little opportunity to spend time at the coast, so he had to make the most of it.

What a night. Ben, usually so cocksure and confident, had been nervous about contacting Daniel. They both had. Why? He didn't understand. All that fear seemed pointless now. Daniel was a terrific guy. But then, he always had been. What made them think fame would have changed him? Despite his success, the leading-man role, the ritzy hotel, he was as grounded as the boy they used to know. None of it had gone to his head.

He'd changed in other ways. Subtle ways. Probably not even obvious to anyone who didn't know him before. His confidence had taken a knock. Not as a performer — Daniel was an absolute star, matching Max LaFranchi beat for beat. But off stage, there were moments of hesitancy. A flicker of uncertainty in his eyes. A slight mistrust of Ben and Christian to begin with.

Christian doubted Daniel even knew of it and didn't blame him.

What happened on that ship had taken its toll, mentally and physically. Oliver had fucked him up.

What a piece of shit the man was. He always has been. A poisonous, spiteful little bitch, even when he was a kid.

No wonder Daniel was wary after what Oliver had done. Jesus, Christian wouldn't want to speak to any of them if it had happened to him. Thankfully, Daniel had been open to their approach.

And it was good to see him again. Overload was unfinished business for them all. Tonight wasn't the time to discuss it, but tomorrow they would have to talk.

That was the reason he and Ben were here, after all. To see the show, yes, but that wasn't everything.

As he approached the waterfront, the fresh breeze rippled through Christian's hair. He turned his face into the wind, taking full advantage. Farther down the promenade, the lights of the famous Blackpool illuminations lit up the Golden Mile like the Las Vegas strip.

He would have to come back here sometime. *Bring Lars and the kids. They will love the spectacle and magic.*

Now it was late, and he was tired. Tomorrow would bring its own challenges.

Christian turned north and walked toward the hotel.

If the wind was blowing in another direction, he might have heard the footsteps coming up behind him.

But Christian knew nothing until a heavy blow struck the back of his head.

One sudden moment of indescribable pain before his vision blurred.

Faded.

Then there was nothing.

Chapter Eight

Elijah woke refreshed. He hadn't expected to sleep so well the night before the final challenge, especially after his conversation with Keeley in the bar. But the minute he turned out the light, he'd gone straight off, not stirring until his seven-thirty alarm call. He yawned and stretched in the double bed, pushing his limbs into the cool outer reaches.

One more night of sleeping on his own, then he'd be back with Daniel, sharing the same bed. When he rolled over in the dark, reaching out, Daniel would be there. God, how he missed him.

The thought of seeing him was more exciting than winning this competition.

But no, that was what he was here for. To win. If he could hold his focus for one more day, it would all be over and he would return to Daniel a winner.

Rolling out of bed, he took a moment in the semi-darkness to remember the layout of the room. *Damn hotels. You never know where you are when you first get up.*

Naked, he headed to the bathroom and relieved himself.

He ran his beard trimmer over his stubble while the shower heated. It wouldn't hurt to look tidy today. If he lifted the trophy, his photo would appear in all the prominent papers, magazines and news sites when the episode aired, which made it worth a little extra effort this morning.

Freshly showered, he put on clean underpants and ordered breakfast from room service. Nothing heavy, just coffee, juice and an English muffin with butter. He had no appetite but would force it down. He didn't want to lose focus later just because he was hungry.

His mobile rang as he pulled up his jeans.

Daniel's face flashed on the caller ID.

"Morning, sexy," he answered with a smile.

"Good morning to you, *Top Cook* champion," Daniel said.

"Not yet, I'm not."

"You will be. I'm just calling to wish you luck, but I know you won't need it. You'll win, regardless."

"I wish I had your faith."

"I've got enough for both of us," Daniel said. "If you cook like you did on Sunday, you can't fail."

Elijah sat on the end of the bed and closed his eyes, happy just to hear his voice. "How was last night? Good show?"

"It was. There are only a few performances left. I think everyone wants to make the most of it. But that's not all, I got a surprise after the show."

"Oh, yeah?"

"Two of the boys from Overload came backstage to visit."

Elijah froze. Something tightened in his guts. "Overload?"

"Relax," Daniel said smoothly. "These guys are *nothing* like Oliver. They never were. Ben and Christian, they couldn't be nicer. I'm glad they made the effort to get in touch. It's something I should have done myself a long time ago."

"Will they be around for long?" Elijah asked, still suspicious.

"I don't know. I'm meeting them for lunch late and I'll find out. If they're still here tomorrow, you can meet them yourself. Then you'll stop fretting."

"I'm not fretting," he lied.

"I can hear it in your voice. There's no need. Ben and Christian are good guys. There's no malice in either of them. Now, how about you? All ready for today?"

"As ready as I'll ever be."

"Good. Knock 'em dead. You're always a winner to me."

When he entered the hotel lobby for the obligatory photo call and to film his fake arrival at the venue, the first thing Elijah heard was Keeley swearing at Pascal, the production assistant.

"I don't want that cheap, shitty brand. I want the items specified on my fucking ingredient list," Keeley raged.

"It's the same thing." Pascal spoke slowly, as though giving instructions to a senile old lady. "The brand you wanted wasn't available."

"*Make it available.*"

"There isn't time, you'll just have to make do. These are perfectly adequate replacements."

"Make do. Make-fucking-do. Are you trying to set me up? Do you want me to lose? Is that it? Is this just a big fucking fix for one of the boys to win?"

"Nothing is set up," Pascal said wearily. "We've had to substitute alternative ingredients with Elijah and Joshua too."

"You see," Elijah said, intervening. "No harm done. We're all in the same position."

Pascal used the diversion to make a speedy exit.

"That bitch has had it in for me since the start," Kelley seethed, jabbing a bony finger toward the retreating assistant.

"And you being so lovely with her," Elijah remarked. "I can't imagine *why* she wouldn't like you. C'mon, outside. You need to top up your nicotine levels. The world will seem like a nicer place when you do."

He took her elbow and escorted her out the front door. She didn't resist.

It was a beautiful morning with the sun already climbing a cloudless blue sky. Elijah could only imagine how hot it would get around midday. He hoped the kitchens were well ventilated.

Keeley shoved a cigarette in her mouth and clicked her lighter. She inhaled deeply.

"Better?" he asked with a smile.

She blew smoke in his face and nodded. "Give any more thought to my offer?"

"The book? No. There's nothing to think about."

She narrowed her eyes, scrutinizing him. He found her gaze too intense and looked away.

"I don't know what your problem is," she said. "You've read my account of the Durham Strangler. You know I'm not a hack. My books are painstakingly researched and highly praised accounts of true crime.

I'm a respected journalist. I won't do a hatchet job on this."

"But you only got involved in the Durham case because you *were* planning to write a hatchet job on one of the survivors." Elijah had also done his research. Keeley had wanted to write an expose on Dale Zachery, a closeted actor at the time. She'd been on the set of his TV series, digging for dirt, and if she hadn't been snooping around his private life, she would never have encountered the killer.

"That's not *strictly* true. Let's just say I was in the right place at the right time."

"Maybe you were, that time. But you weren't on the *Anthem*. You have no direct involvement or experience of what went down."

"So? I'm a writer," she said brightly, punching the cigarette in his direction. "I do research. I investigate. No detail is too small. As a matter of fact, I've already started work on the *Anthem* case."

Jesus, she doesn't know when to quit. Whatever failings she might have, lack of resolve wasn't one of them. "The answer's still no. Do yourself a favor and find another subject."

"I don't think so," she said airily. "There's a story there. A big one. And I intend to be the one who writes it."

* * * *

Max slid against the hot, hard body in bed beside her. She should be exhausted. She'd had so little sleep, but wow, she felt totally energized. It was a long time since she'd slept with a man, and what a man to break the drought. *What a body*. She slid her hand around Ben's tight waist, making for his soft, slumbering cock.

"Enough," he protested lightly. "I'm worn out."

Max pressed a kiss on his shoulder instead. *Poor baby*. She had gone pretty hard on him. She didn't know what had come over her. When she had met him in the bar, she'd acted like another woman. A character. Not herself at all. One-night stands — if that was what this was — had never been her thing. Never. In her entire life, she hadn't gone to bed with a man so soon after meeting him. *Like the same night*.

It's awful.

No, it's wonderful.

Once they'd gotten to her room, she couldn't get enough of him. Of his hot young body and hard cock.

'How old are you?' she'd whispered as he hustled her against the wall, his hands tearing at her clothes.

'Thirty-two,' he'd murmured, pressing a trail of kissing along her neck, driving her insane.

Another first. She had been with younger men, four or five years younger than she. But a twenty-two-year age difference, that was something else. *Why does he want me?* she'd wondered as he'd slipped his hands inside her panties. Then she had been past the point of caring.

It had lasted all night. He'd made love with a skill and stamina entirely unknown, leading to one orgasm after another.

By morning she had been shattered but still wanting more.

Max LaFranchi having a one-night stand with a black man more than twenty years her junior. The thought made her smile. The press would have a shit-fit if they got wind of it. They'd drag out hideous photos of her as a teenager to run beside salacious speculation about Ben. Like she gave a toss. She'd given up caring what they wrote about her years ago. Eating disorders, mental breakdowns and career catastrophes — the press had lapped it up in the past. They would again, given a chance.

Max rolled out of bed and hurried to the bathroom. Despite everything he'd done to her, she was curiously shy about Ben seeing her naked. She must look a fright. No man had seen her in the morning in a long time. One glance in the mirror confirmed her fears. She was a hot mess. In too much of a hurry to drag Ben into bed to worry about taking off her makeup. What a sight — hair all over the place and lipstick smeared halfway across her face. She grabbed a cleansing cloth and set about removing it.

"Tranny roadkill," she said to her reflection.

Despite her appearance, she smiled. Why shouldn't she? A hot young man had taken her to bed and fucked her brains out. *How many fifty-four-year-old women waking up this morning can claim that?*

Max laughed and ran the shower.

Ten minutes later she returned to the bedroom wearing a silk robe and her hair wound in a towel.

Ben lay naked in the ruin of the bedclothes. He was propped up on pillows. He smiled, dimples in situ.

"Some night, eh?"

Max opened the curtains. "It sure was."

"Do you have to go someplace?"

She turned to look at him. The pull he had on her was almost magnetic. She could drop the robe and towel right now and climb back into bed, ready to ravish him all over again. "Afraid I do. I've got a fundraising thing with Daniel this morning. Got to put the war paint on.

They'll expect the full Max LaFranchi experience — tits, teeth and dancing feet."

"And I'm the one who got a private performance."

"Yeah," she said carefully, sitting on the edge of the bed. "Listen. Last night... I don't usually do that kind of thing."

"Max —"

"I mean, we'd only just met. I don't know what came over me. I wouldn't —"

"Max," he said firmly, "you don't have to say anything."

"It's just..."

"I had a wonderful night. The best. I hope you did too."

Her face grew hot. *Oh, crap.* She was blushing. "I did."

"No regrets?"

"Oh, God no."

"Then nothing else matters, does it?"

The man was really something. Smart, sexy, kind, considerate — an out-of-this-world lover.

"You are my first one-night stand," she admitted. "Ever."

"Was it a one-night stand?" he inquired softly. The smile had gone.

"Oh," she said. "I just assumed... You wouldn't..."

He rolled across the bed, seemingly unconcerned, unashamed of his nakedness, and took her hand. "I don't know what happens next. But I'll be around for a few more days at least. Why don't we see how things go?"

"All right."

"And you can still be the lady who never had a one-night stand."

Max threw back her head and laughed. "Well, if it's my reputation at stake, I can hardly refuse."

"There's something else," Ben said. He rose onto his knees, revealing his huge dick jutting proudly from between his thighs. "I've made a rousing recovery."

He threw his arms around Max and pulled her down onto the bed.

A smile and a hard-on, how can I refuse?

* * * *

Pete Jericho and Bruce Brooks sat side by side at their judging table in the grand hall of The McDonald Hotel. Most of the room had been partitioned off to give a more intimate feel to the production. Elijah's three plates of food were already positioned in front of them, ready for inspection.

He'd cooked the exact same dinner he'd served to Daniel on Sunday evening, only he'd refined it further. He didn't know how he'd done it, or where the skill for presentation came from. Watching *Top Cook*, both the celebrity and standard versions of the show for all these years, must have taught him something. Perhaps it came through osmosis and he'd taken it in without consciously realizing.

What he'd assembled on those plates looked truly professional. Beautiful.

The director called action and the cameras turned toward him.

Elijah ambled through the room to take his seat in front of the judges. His nerves were shot. There was nothing to be nervous about. Not anymore. He'd done all he could. Whatever came next was out of his control.

He was calmer now than at any other stage of the competition.

"Stunning," Pete said, gesturing toward the plates in front of him. "Absolutely stunning. Your presentation has come so far since you first joined us. You were always a good cook, but tended to slop it on a plate at the start."

"It's my natural greed," Elijah joked.

"There's a nothing slopped out here today," Bruce said in agreement. "This looks superb. You should be proud of yourself."

They pulled the first plate toward them — his starter of crispy fish cakes wrapped in bacon. The food was stone cold. It took so long to set up between shots that the dishes were always cold by the time the judges came to taste them. Obvious really, but not something he'd ever thought of before taking part. Pete and Bruce always took the temperature into account when scoring any of the menus and wouldn't mark anyone down for it.

"Delicious."

"Out of this world."

Elijah couldn't stop smiling. He knew he'd look like a grinning idiot when the episode aired but he didn't care. It meant so much, knowing they enjoyed his food.

Pete and Bruce were equally happy with his main course, the venison fillet. Elijah couldn't image it tasted that good, having gone cold, but the judges loved it, praising him for the way he'd cooked the meat.

He scored a perfect hat-trick with his final dish, the dessert of chocolate raspberry pudding. The judges didn't criticize a single thing across the three courses. They loved everything about his menu.

And that was it. They directed him to wait in another room, out of earshot, while they judged Keeley's and Joshua's dishes. His *Top Cook* journey was almost at an end. As he waited, with the cameras running to catch every flicker of tension in his face, he found he no longer cared about winning. It had been a once-in-a-lifetime experience. Something he couldn't have found elsewhere. So what if he didn't win? It was worth everything just to have taken part.

Joshua ambled in twenty minutes later. The boy tried to act cool, especially in front of the cameras, but Elijah could see it in the brightness of his eyes, in the pink flush of his cheeks.

"Happy?" he asked.

Joshua flopped heavily on the sofa beside him. "I think so. I can't even remember what they said now. The last three hours are a blur. Intense, man."

"I know what you mean. And how fast they went, wow."

When Keeley came to join them, she too was smiling. "Can't believe I've got so much emotion invested in a few fucking plates of food. Me."

The cameraman tutted.

"When this goes out, I don't think you'll have a single line that they don't bleep," Elijah said.

"Like I give a fuck," she snarled directly into the nearest camera. "One. Flying. Fuck."

From there it was a waiting game. The judges had to discuss the merits of their individual courses before a decision could be made about the winner. Elijah, Keeley and Joshua waited where they were until they were summoned back into the dining room.

"Can't I go for a cigarette?" Keeley snapped.

"No," the assistant director told her. "It won't take long, and we need you all ready to go when we get the call."

"It's a goddamn cookery show," she said. "We're not waiting on the verdict for mass murder. We cooked some food, they ate it and they liked it — big deal."

"Chill out," Elijah told her. "You can smoke all the cigarettes you like later, when you lose."

"Oh, you'd like that, wouldn't you? Well, listen up, sucker. Keeley Rank doesn't lose. Never has and she's not about to start."

After a long hour, which seemed even longer, they got word from one of the runners — the judges had made their decision. The camera crew gathered around the contestants to film their walk back to the dining room. Elijah's insides were in turmoil. It was the most nerve-racking thing he'd ever done. Every footstep seemed like a mile.

Pete and Bruce stood on their marks in the main hall. Elijah and the others moved in front of them. It seemed another interminable age as they got all the cameras into position. His insides growled and he hoped they wouldn't catch it on sound.

He closed his eyes and took deep breaths.

"This has been one of the most difficult decisions we've ever had to make," Pete said, egging the tension.

"The standard has been higher than any previous *Top Cook* competition," Bruce said, laying it on thick.

Elijah dug his fingernails into his palms. *Oh, God, did I do enough? Probably not. It won't be me. Fish cakes, what was I thinking? Far too simple. They're gonna say Keeley. And she'll deserve it.*

"Our champion, our *Celebrity Top Cook* is…"

They dragged it out. The pause went on forever.

"Elijah."

Suddenly Keeley and Joshua had their arms around him. They bounced around and congratulated him.

He'd done it. Unbelievably, he'd done it. *It can't be right. They must have made a mistake.* But as Bruce and Pete thrust the trophy into his hands, Elijah realized it was true.

He was the winner of *Celebrity Top Cook*.

* * * *

Daniel waited for Max at the front of the hotel. Their car, a long black Mercedes, idled in the parking bay. The early September sky was blue and cloudless, but the heat of the sun was tempered by a refreshing breeze off the Irish Sea.

Daniel checked his phone for the eighth time in as many minutes. Still no message from Elijah. *What is taking so long? They're due to serve their final three courses for lunch. Why haven't the judges decided yet?*

Take it easy, he told himself. They had no guarantee Elijah would win. Daniel thought his cooking was the best—that didn't mean the judges would agree. *What the hell?* Elijah had made it to the final. If he didn't win, that was still amazing.

Daniel had been briefed on what to expect today. The cast of *Lady Lynda* were attending an event outside the Blackpool Tower to raise awareness for a local mental health charity. They had to sing a few songs, talk to the TV and radio stations and do whatever they could to boost the profile of the organization.

The cause meant a lot to Daniel and Max. He'd been through enough dark moments of his own this last year to appreciate the importance of good mental health support. He'd been lucky. He had his family and friends and the unfaltering love of Elijah to help him through the difficult days. Not everyone was so fortunate.

Max had made no secret of her own psychological troubles in the past. Eating disorders, physical and emotional breakdowns in her teens and twenties. She'd been sectioned more than once at the height of her difficulties. It was a long time ago. She was over it, a different woman now, but she admitted that she couldn't have recovered without help. This event today was important to both of them.

He was also looking forward to seeing Ben and Christian later. They'd barely scratched the surface last night. There were so many questions he needed to ask. That period of his life, the Overload days, had been a closed box for the last year. Maybe now he should open it and see what was in there.

"Good morning." Max breezed out of the hotel in a cloud of perfume, her smile brighter than the unseasonable September sun.

"Morning," Daniel said. "No need to ask *you* what's so good about it."

"I'm too old to blush about things like that," Max said airily.

She looked fantastic in skintight jeans and a waist-length blue jacket. She'd added a touch of bling with diamond earrings, necklace, bracelets and rings. Her face had been made up for the public, but beneath the powder and gloss, he could see her skin was radiant.

"I'm just jealous," he said. "Pay me a visit on Thursday morning and I'll definitely sport a similar look."

"*Just fucked*," she said. "It's better than any beauty treatment I can recommend. Someone should market it."

Laughing, they climbed into the back of the waiting car.

"I have to take the long way around," the driver told them. "The road is closed up past North Pier."

"What is it this time?" Daniel asked.

"I'm not sure," he replied. "Talk among the cabbies says they found a body that way earlier this morning. But nothing has been confirmed. It could just be that — talk."

"This town sure has its share of accidents," Max said.

"Always has," the driver agreed. "People come here for a good time, but excessive alcohol and an accessible seafront don't make for a good mix. The currents and riptides just off the beach are fatal. I can't count the number of folk who've been carried away."

"That's awful," Daniel said. He thought again of Oliver and his untimely death in the stormy Atlantic. Despite conflicting feelings over him, he couldn't think of a worse way to go. Cold, frightened, fighting hopelessly against the elements. Man was no match for the forces of nature.

The car arrived at the foot of the Blackpool Tower, where a huge crowd had gathered in front of a temporary stage. There had to be a few thousand people there.

"Whoa, I thought this was just a small thing," Daniel said.

Max shrugged. "I must admit, I didn't pay much attention to the details when the offer came in. I just saw the cause and said I'd do it. But so what? You can never have too big an audience."

They got out of the car to huge applause. Daniel felt like a fraud. The crowd behaved as if two movie stars had just arrived, not a couple of old hoofers who'd been playing the Winter Gardens all season. He put his arm around Max and leaned in as dozens of cameras flashed.

"Unbelievable," he said through teeth that were fixed in a huge smile.

"Fucking fabulous," Max said through equally gritted teeth.

Rachel Lopez and Alisha Cameron, their director and producer, stepped forward to join the photo lineup, before leading them off to meet the heads of the charity.

The next hour passed in a blur. He shook hands and met new people with no time to register their names, before he was hurried on to speak to local radio reporters. Thankfully their questions were simple and on-topic.

"What does a charity like this mean to you?"

"How important is mental health?"

"Why do charities need your support?"

He answered whatever they put to him with no difficulty, but if he'd known how big a deal this event was, he'd have come better-prepared.

With barely a pause, he hurried to the stage where the ensemble and orchestra from the show were waiting. He launched straight into one of his numbers. His voice hadn't warmed up but sounded good enough. The crowd was behind him from the start, singing along, swaying their arms in the air. There was a huge amount of goodwill in the town for the show. The local people had taken them to heart.

He stepped down from the stage, making way for Max. She whipped them up with a few bawdy jokes and comments before launching into the dance remix of her song *Roses and Rainbows*. Standing at the side, Daniel laughed as she turned up the camp factor. The audience loved it.

Suddenly a hand grabbed his arm, breaking the spell. Daniel turned.

Ben stood right beside him.

"Hey," he said, before noticing Ben's grim expression.

Ben spoke, but his words were lost beneath the deafening beat of Max's track.

He gripped Daniel's arm tighter and pulled him away from the stage. They hurried around the back.

"What's the matter?" Daniel asked once he could hear.

Before he spoke, Daniel knew the news was bad. Ben's face said it all.

"It's Christian…"

Then Daniel knew with unqualified certainty what the next words would be. Something heavy and cold gripped his insides, dragging downward, a weight of indomitable horror.

"He's dead," Ben said. "Christian is dead. He's been murdered."

In that moment, the emotional security Daniel had tried all year to construct around himself crumbled to nothing.

Chapter Nine

There was a rushing sound in Daniel's ears, as if the ocean roared through his head. His pulse raced faster and his breath grew shallow. He looked at Ben and his features swam in and out of focus. Ben slipped an arm around his waist and led him toward the tower entrance.

"Is there somewhere quiet we can go?" Ben asked a passing official.

"At the top of the stairs, turn left. There's a green room set out for the reception later. Do you want me to show you?" the uniformed woman asked.

"We'll find it. Thanks." Ben tugged Daniel's arm. "C'mon, let's go."

The room on the first floor was huge. Trestle tables ran along one wall, set with a vast buffet, the food still covered in cling film. Ben spotted a selection of drinks and snatched a bottle of mineral water.

"Drink this. Slowly."

Daniel did what he said. His tongue and the roof of his mouth were bone dry.

Gradually, his senses came back into focus.

From the window, he could see the stage below and the crowd of people who danced excitedly and sang along, enjoying the party, all eyes on Max. It felt to Daniel as if his world had stopped, but just there, meters away, life went on.

"What happened?" he asked at last.

Ben shook his head. "I don't know exactly. I spent the night at your hotel. I didn't leave until ten this morning. When I got back to our place, the cops were already there. They told me Christian was dead."

Daniel's brain worked slowly, struggling to fit the pieces together. He remembered what the taxi driver had said earlier. "The body on the beach? That was Christian?"

Ben nodded. "I think so. They wouldn't say much. The cops were more interested in asking questions than answering any of mine. But yes, they found him this morning. Somewhere on the beach."

"Could it have been an accident?" Daniel knew the answer but asked anyway. Christian had had a few drinks last night but hadn't been drunk when he'd left the hotel. Not even close.

"They're treating his death as suspicious," Ben said. "Which means they're treating it as murder."

Murder.

Daniel's world was shrinking and a pounding noise filled his head again. He put a hand against the wall to keep from falling over. *This can't be real. Not again.*

"Could it... was it...a robbery gone wrong?" he asked.

"It doesn't look like it." Ben took out his phone. His hands shook as he tapped through the menu screen. "The cops didn't say much but it's all over social media. A few people got a look at his body before the police arrived. It might just be bullshit, I hope to God it is, but they're talking about it being some kind of ritualistic murder."

"What?" Daniel felt more detached with every moment. Ben's words came from a distant place and behind him, Max still sang about roses and rainbows to a disco beat.

Ben put his phone away. He closed his eyes and took a breath before speaking. "They say...they're saying his heart was removed."

Daniel fell against the wall. His legs lost their strength and he slid down to the floor. "What does that even mean?"

"I don't know," Ben mumbled. "It might be nothing. Talk on the internet. Rumors. But the police were cagey when they spoke to me. I think they were holding something back."

Christian is dead. This can't be happening. I must be dreaming. I'm still in bed. None of this is real.

Ben went back to the drinks table and grabbed two bottles of beer from the ice bucket. He ripped off the caps and sat on the floor beside Daniel, passing him a bottle.

"I could do with something stronger, but this will have to do," he said.

They both drank.

"I must have been one of the last people to see him alive," Daniel said. "If not *the* last."

Apart from whoever killed him.

"The cops will want to talk to you. I'm surprised they haven't already."

"I'd better go back to the hotel. If they're retracing Christian's steps, that's where they'll be." Daniel took another sip of beer. He wasn't ready to move. He doubted he had the strength to stand. Images of Christian filled his head. How he'd looked last night, as they said goodbye in the foyer, making plans for today. "He wanted to meet for lunch," Daniel said. "The three of us."

Ben wiped his eyes. "It's fucked up. So fucked up."

Daniel leaned closer and put his arm around him, giving Ben the release he needed. The tears came unchecked. His body shook, his shoulders heaved. Daniel held him quietly. Nothing he could say would make this better. There were no words.

He thought about Christian's family, his husband Lars, and their children and the hell they'd have to endure today. Just an ordinary morning until they received a knock at the door — two solemn-faced police officers. *I'm afraid we have some bad news.*

Those poor kids. They've lost one family already. How cruel to find happiness and security again, only to have it torn away.

Hot tears rolled down Daniel's face.

At last, Ben pulled it together. He sat up straight, wiping his eyes with the back of his hands. He sighed and finished the rest of his beer.

"There's something else," he said at last.

Daniel wiped his own eyes. "What?"

He took a deep breath. "Christian and me. We didn't come here just to see your show. There's something else we had to talk to you about."

Daniel braced himself. More bad news, he knew it. "Okay."

"Did you hear what happened to Luke?" Ben asked.

"Luke Torrens? No. What did happen?"

Luke Torrens, another core member of Overload. Like the others, Daniel had lost touch with him. He hadn't seen Luke since the band had separated.

"I thought not. You would have mentioned it otherwise. He's dead too."

Another sucker punch, right to the guts.

"What? When? Why didn't you tell me before?"

"We only found out last week."

"When did he die?"

"About six weeks ago."

"And was he...?"

"Murdered? Yes." Ben sighed. "I hadn't seen him in years. I heard along the way he'd gotten married and lived somewhere on the south coast. That was it. Then Christian called me last Wednesday. One of his fans on Twitter sent a link to an online news story. It seems Luke owned a surfing store in Bournemouth. According to the article, he interrupted a robbery and was killed in the process."

"Oh my God."

"We said nothing last night because we didn't want to spoil the reunion. That's what lunch was all about, we were going to tell you today," Ben sneered. "When Christian heard the news, he wanted to reach out to the other boys. Thought it was as good a time as any to forget the past and move forward. After what happened with Luke, and Oliver before him, it was time to bring the boys back together. Not for a group reunion, or any of that shit, but as friends."

Blood pounded in Daniel's temples. It was too much—information overload. In just a few minutes he'd learned that two of his mates were dead. He put his head in his hands. The world had turned to shit.

"Did they catch who was responsible for the robbery?"

"Nah. No one. Only now it's got me thinking..."

Daniel knew what he was going to say.

"What if there was no robbery? What if it was just a front and Luke was killed deliberately?"

It sounded so far-fetched. And yet, of the original members of Overload, six boys if including Oliver, three were dead. All within the space of a year.

"But Oliver killed himself," Daniel said.

"I know. But Luke didn't, and neither did Christian. What if their murders have something to do with Oliver's suicide?"

Daniel shook his head. "It's not possible. There's no way they could be connected. None of us had anything to do with Oliver. It was pure chance that I met him on the *Anthem*. Chance and bad luck. That's all."

"What about family? Someone related who wants to get even."

"Then they would have come after me or someone else from the *Anthem*. Not Christian and Luke. Besides, there's no one. Oliver didn't have any family. He's got an older sister someplace, but I don't think they were close."

"A mad fan then?"

Daniel laughed. It was an empty sound. "He didn't have any fans. He spent his entire life alienating people. Nobody queued up to sing his praises, even after he died. No, I don't believe it. There can't be a connection between any of these guys."

"They were all in Overload," Ben said, throwing up his hands. "That's a pretty big connection."

"It's a coincidence," Daniel said. "Not a connection."

"I hope you're right."

"I do too, because the alternative is unthinkable."

They sat in silence for several minutes. Outside, Max was still on stage, giving the crowd one of her old hits. Daniel listened, latching on to the tune, reaching for an escape. A way out of his troubles, only for a moment. *Isn't that what music is supposed to do?*

Ben sighed heavily and got to his feet. He offered a hand to Daniel and pulled him up.

"Let's go."

"Where?"

"Your hotel. The police will want to see you. Who knows, by now they might be prepared to tell us what happened to Christian."

* * * *

Detective Inspector John Ritson arrived at The Majestic Hotel with Sergeant Dee Holiday. A couple of uniformed officers were stationed in the lobby. At the request of the hotel manager, the police kept their presence low-key. Ritson wouldn't usually pay heed to such demands, but as the victim hadn't been staying here, he decided to cut them some slack. For now at least. The Majestic was the last place Christian Gates had been seen alive. If he needed to turn it into a crime scene, then he would, five-star rating or not.

The hotel manager, Hayley Partridge, a petite, well-dressed redhead, came out from the reception desk to meet him.

"DI Ritson." She held out her hand. "Mr. Blake and Ms. LaFranchi are in their suites. If you'll follow me, I'll take you up."

"Hold it a minute," Ritson said. She was in far too great a hurry to get him out the pubic foyer. He had no problem giving the hotel a certain amount of leeway, but they weren't calling the shots. "Before I speak to them, I want to check out the bar area and see the CCTV footage from last night."

Hayley's business-like smile did not waver, but he could not mistake the ice in her voice. "Certainly, Inspector. Let me show you."

The bar revealed nothing he didn't already know. A team had been through, taking pictures and getting a copy of the security footage. Someone at the station was right now trawling through it frame by frame, checking out the people who Christian had been drinking with, and noting any other guests in the area at the time. Ritson wanted to get a feel for the place before speaking to those involved.

Hayley took Ritson and DS Holiday to the concierge's office where the monitors were installed for the cameras. He raced through the footage at high speed, watching the people in Christian's group and how they interacted with one another. There were no obvious conflicts between them. It all seemed pretty low-key and innocuous. On the surface at least. Ritson learned long ago to dig deeper to find the truth.

Hayley took him to Daniel Blake's suite.

The actor answered the door himself, his face instantly recognizable. Ritson's eldest daughter had dragged him to a matinee of *Lady Lynda* a couple of weeks back, but even if he hadn't seen the show, he would have recognized him. Unlike a lot of the celebrities his daughters were into, Daniel Blake had a far-reaching appeal, as popular with pensioners as with teenagers and equally liked by men and women. Despite his good looks, the public regarded him as a kind of everyman.

Those handsome features were tarnished today. His famous baby blues were red-rimmed and blood shot. His face bore a stunned expression of grief. Ritson knew the expression well — he'd seen it a million times.

"Come in," Daniel said, leading them to the sitting room. "Can I offer you anything? Tea, coffee, something cold?"

"We're fine," Ritson said. "Don't trouble yourself." He quickly took in the suite. It was the swankiest hotel room he'd ever seen. His wife would kill for a night in a place like this. Checking out the leather furnishing, the carpets, the bar, he wondered how much damage a night in this hotel would do to his bank balance. *Too much to even consider it.*

A dark-skinned man sat on the sofa, nursing a drink in a heavy crystal tumbler. *This must be Ben Delaney.* Ritson had studied photos of Overload on the way over. Ben had changed from that fresh-faced, skinny kid in the group photos, they both had, but it was undoubtedly him.

They'd already given initial statements to uniformed officers. Ritson explained that he wanted to go over the finer details.

"Can you tell us anything about what happened yet?" Daniel asked.

"The stuff they're saying on here." Ben brandished his phone. "Is any of it true?"

Ritson stiffened. *Goddamn social media.* When he had started his career, they only had to worry about neighborhood gossip. It used to take days, sometimes weeks, for a rumor to catch on. These days, the stories were circulating within hours. Most often sooner.

"I haven't read any of that nonsense," Ritson said. "You'd do well to ignore it too. Some people have a malicious streak. They get off on spreading lies. Anything to cause offense."

"What happened to Christian?" Daniel asked.

"Mr. Gates' husband is on his way to make a formal identification of the body. Until he does, we need to keep any speculation at a minimum."

"But it is Christian? You're sure of that?"

"Yes," Ritson answered. "From the personal items found on the body, and the CCTV images we've seen, there no doubt. Identification is just a formality at this stage."

"Shit," Ben swore. "I've had hours to get my head around this and I still can't believe it."

"What about the mutilations to the body?" Daniel asked. "Is all that true?"

"There were mutilations, yes," Ritson said carefully, watching each of their reactions.

Ben looked as if he were about to be sick. Though experience had taught the DI to maintain the old maxim—that everyone was a suspect—in truth, these two were pretty much ruled out. Ben said he'd been with Max LaFranchi all night, a story she'd already corroborated to one of the uniforms. Though Daniel didn't have the luxury of such an alibi, the hotel's security footage had him going to his room, where he'd remained for the rest of the night. Unless he'd climbed out of the window and scaled five floors all the way down and back again, his story was also tight.

"Is the ritual part true?" Ben asked.

Ritson's mouth tightened. *What the hell are these people saying online? Jesus, have pity on the boy's family*, he thought. *They shouldn't have to learn this stuff from a retweet.* "We don't think so, no."

"Why not?"

"The mutilation of the body, we believe it was more personal in nature."

Daniel and Ben exchanged a look. It was quick, but so was Ritson.

"What aren't you two telling me?" he asked.

"What aren't you telling us?" Daniel said firmly. "*How* was it personal?"

It went against every professional principle, but he told them what they wanted to know. Better it came from him than a Chinese whisper. "All right," he said, "I'll tell you. The killer cut out Christian's heart and placed it in his mouth."

"Oh, my god," Daniel gasped.

"Fuck." Ben sighed, putting his head in both of his hands.

"So what aren't you telling me?" Ritson asked.

"It's…it's…" Daniel's mouth gaped open and closed like a floundering fish. "I didn't think there could be a connection when Ben told me, but now I don't know what to think."

Ritson clenched his fists. "Your friend is dead. Tell me what you know and I'll decide whether there's a connection."

Daniel crossed the room and sat next to Ben. He put his arm on his shoulder. "Tell him what you told me."

Ben drew a breath and told him about Luke Torrens, another member of the band who had recently turned up dead. Ritson shivered with unease as the story unfolded. The cases seemed unconnected, but his copper's sixth sense told him otherwise. He knew from experience to trust it. When Ben finished, Ritson's mind was on red alert.

He turned to DS Holiday. "Get onto Bournemouth, now. Find out everything there is on the Luke Torrens case. I want it all."

She jumped to attention, hurrying out of the door with her phone in her hand.

"So, you do think these deaths are related?" Daniel asked.

"At this stage in an investigation, I consider all the options. Have either of you two received any threats?"

"No."

"Nothing."

"What about social media? Any suspicious activity? Trolls, that kind of thing."

Ben shook his head.

"I don't really have anything to do with all that," Daniel said. "I can't be bothered with it. My manager has an office assistant who posts stuff on my behalf. I don't get involved."

"I want your manager's contact details. We need to look into everything. There were five of you in that group, right? Well, I count four. Where's the other boy?"

"David Kharsa," Ben said. "He lives in America."

"Do you know how to find him?"

"No, I haven't heard from him in years."

"Sorry," Daniel said, holding up his hand. "It's taking me a while to process all of this. But it sounds like you believe the murders are connected to our band. Do you think we're in danger?"

"All options." Ritson shrugged.

"He's right," Ben said, looking at Daniel squarely. "It sounds crazy, but we have to face it. There might be someone out there who wants to kill the surviving members of Overload. They were in Blackpool last night and are probably still here now."

Daniel nodded grimly. "And so are we."

Chapter Ten

The three and a half hours on the train from Edinburgh were among the longest of Elijah's life, compounded by a delay leaving the station that almost caused him to miss his connection in Preston. Thankfully he'd made it and was now on the last, short leg of the journey. The whole focus of his day had changed with a phone call from Daniel late that afternoon.

Elijah had completed his filming commitments for *Celebrity Top Cook* and was in his room, resting ahead of the wrap party when Daniel rang.

Everything stopped in that moment.

Daniel tried to play it down, as if the murders of his old band mates were just an awful coincidence, but Elijah heard the truth in his voice. It was a front, nothing but bravado. Elijah didn't believe in coincidences, not like that. Two guys wearing the same shirt to a party — that was a coincidence. But two members of the same group being killed a few weeks apart, no way.

"I'm coming back," he said.

Elijah had hurriedly thrown his stuff into his suitcase and raced to the station. He called Pascal from the taxi to let her know he couldn't attend the party.

"Elijah, come on, you're the champion," she complained. "You *have* to be there."

"Sorry, it's a family emergency. I'm leaving now."

He hung up before she could protest further. He didn't want to hear it.

One moment he'd been wallowing in success, the next he was deep in a nightmare.

The train's wi-fi was patchy. He tried logging on to the news whenever he caught a signal, eventually finding the website for Blackpool's local paper. The body of a young man found dead on the beach that morning was the lead story. The details were sketchy. The police had yet to confirm the identity of the victim, or the circumstances of his death. Sadness for a man he had never met overwhelmed him as he read the news, followed by anger, and finally fear.

Christian Gates had gone to Blackpool to reunite with his old band mates. He'd been murdered hours later.

As Elijah read the story again and tried to make sense of it, his thoughts kept coming back to a single, insidious idea.

This has something to do with Oliver Gill.

Rationally, he knew there couldn't be a connection. Christian's death had nothing to do with that night on the *Anthem*. Oliver was dead, for Christ's sake. Elijah didn't believe in ghosts or revenge from the grave. Christian was simply in the wrong place at the wrong time. That was all it could be.

The worst kind of luck.

And yet, Elijah couldn't convince himself that was true. *Three men from Overload died within a year of each other. There's nothing suspicious about that? Like fuck there isn't.*

All he knew for certain was he had to get back to Daniel, as soon as possible.

The train made it into Blackpool at nine thirty and he caught a taxi from the rank outside. "The Majestic Hotel," he told the driver.

Once there he paid the fare and hurried inside, his heart racing. When he saw Daniel, had his assurance he was okay, then he could relax.

"Elijah." The voice came from the direction of the reception desk. "Mr. Mann, hi."

It was the young man who regularly worked the desk at night. Elijah didn't remember his name. The boy beckoned him over.

"I'm in a hurry," Elijah told him.

"Mr. Blake told me to expect you. Welcome back." He smiled.

"Thanks, but I want to go straight up," Elijah said. "It's been a long day."

"Hasn't it though," the boy sounded excited. "You've heard about the murder, right? They called me into work early tonight to speak to the cops. I was one of the last people to see the dead guy alive. In here. In the bar, last night. I watched him walk out that door, never to be seen again."

"That's terrible, really, but I want to see Daniel," Elijah said impatiently. "Excuse me."

"That's what I'm trying to tell you," the man said, handing over a pass key. "He's not here. He said to tell you he'd be back around eleven."

"Did he say where he's going?"

"To the theater. For the show, of course."

"The show? What the..." Elijah sighed. Daniel shouldn't have gone on tonight. *What was he thinking?* "Okay, thanks. I'll dump my cases and head straight there. Could you get a taxi to be outside in five minutes?"

"Mr. Blake, er...Daniel, he said you should wait upstairs. He's not expecting you at the theater."

"Five minutes," he insisted and hurried for the lift. He'd spent the entire evening stuck on a train, helpless—he'd be damned if he would sit around here doing nothing. He wanted to be with Daniel. Now.

Elijah sighed with relief when the taxi pulled up outside of the theater and he saw a uniformed police officer at the stage door. At least someone had the sense to keep an eye on Daniel. The cops must believe there was a risk to put a watch on him. It didn't make it any easier, but at least the police were doing something.

The stage door attendant recognized him and took him straight to Daniel's dressing room.

"Terrible business," the man said, leading him through the narrow corridors.

"I didn't expect he'd go on tonight."

"Neither did we. As soon as she heard the news, Rachel told the understudy to prepare. But Daniel insisted. Good of 'im, I say. There'd be a lot of disappointed folks in the audience if they didn't see 'im. Daniel and Max, well, they're what people paid their money for, ain't they?"

A burly guy stood guard outside Daniel's dressing room. Thickset and muscular, he had sleeve tattoos down both forearms and the stance of a professional bouncer.

"We've increased security inside the theater," the manager explained. "Just as a precaution, till the police know what's going on."

"Have there been any direct threats to Daniel or the cast? Anonymous letters, parcels, that sort of thing?"

He shook his head. "Nothing. Max had a few saucy messages a couple of weeks back but she says it's par for the course. She always gets her share of mucky letters during a long run. Nothing to lose sleep over."

Elijah nodded and went inside.

A monitor was mounted on the dressing room wall, screening live action from the stage as the cast threw themselves into the finale. If Daniel was concerned about his safety, it didn't come across in his performance. He was in fine voice, confident and strong, and the audience responded joyfully, applauding every line.

Elijah relaxed for the first time since receiving Daniel's call.

He stood just watching the screen till he assured himself that Daniel was fine, then took a vodka from the mini bar. He sat down but kept his eyes trained on the performance until the end of the show.

The final applause was booming. The vibrations from the auditorium extended all the way back here. Elijah smiled, finally relieved. And proud of Daniel's professionalism. Nothing could put him off his game. The audience had paid to see him and he gave them full value, never less than one hundred percent.

Elijah knew he couldn't have done the same under the circumstances.

When the applause died, and Daniel came through the door, Elijah leaped to his feet to meet him.

"What are you doing here?" Daniel asked, rushing forward, throwing his arms around him.

Elijah embraced him deeply, burrowing his face into his neck. "Are you kidding? I couldn't wait another minute. I was so afraid for you."

He put his hand on the back of Daniel's head and drew him in for a kiss. He closed his eyes, breathing him in, holding him, taking comfort from his body. He was safe. Thank God, he was safe.

"Are you sure you're all right?" Elijah asked at last, leaning back to look at him, searching his face for signs of stress.

He nodded. "I'm fine. Really."

"I'm not leaving you alone again. Not until we know what's going on. Jesus, have the police given you any information?"

"Not yet." Daniel spotted his drink. "That looks good. Vodka? Would you pour me one while I get out of this costume?"

"Anything you want." Elijah crossed to the fridge and fixed his drink. He drained his own and poured another double measure. "I can't believe you did the show. Why didn't you let the understudy go on?"

Daniel sat at the dressing table and removed the microphone wires from his hair. "And do what? Sit around the hotel on my own? Stare at the walls and go crazy?"

"There's a cop at the stage door. They must think you're in some kind of danger. Haven't they advised you to lay low?"

"It's a precaution. I don't think they have any ideas yet. Besides, on stage in front of thousands of people — that's probably the safest place in town. Nothing can happen to me here. Not that I think anything will happen."

Daniel took off his shirt and hung it up. He came across the room toward Elijah, bare chested, looking hairy and hot. He straddled Elijah's lap. Elijah's hands went instinctively to his tight waist, pressing his thumbs into the cut muscle. All he wanted was to hold him.

Daniel leaned forward and placed a soft kiss on his forehead. "Congratulations, *Celebrity Top Cook*."

Elijah laughed hollowly. "That seems kind of trivial now."

"It's not trivial. It's a big deal. I'm proud of you. You deserve it."

Elijah knew Daniel too well. He was deflecting, and he couldn't really blame him. Whatever it took for him to process this crazy shit was fine. He would talk when he wanted to. That wasn't now.

Elijah slid his hands around Daniel's waist, moving lower to cup his buttocks. "I'm taking you back to the hotel. Where I can look after you. I want you to myself."

"That's exactly what I want."

They were interrupted by a knock at the door. Daniel's dresser, Joe, entered without waiting for a reply. The boy stopped short when he saw the two of them on the chair, Daniel bare-chested with Elijah's hands on his butt.

"Oh, s-sorry." The boy blushed furiously. "I didn't know you were back, Elijah. I'll...come for the clothes later."

Daniel climbed off Elijah's lap. "It's okay, Joe, come in. The sooner I get this stuff off, the sooner I can go home."

The boy loitered in the doorway. His face burned scarlet. "If you're sure," Joe said. His hands shook as he closed the door behind him and he almost tripped as he approached the dresser.

Elijah picked up his drink and moved to the sofa, allowing Daniel and Joe to do what they had to do at the dressing table. Daniel shuffled out of his trousers without a trace of embarrassment. Like most actors, he wasn't self-conscious about undressing in front of other people. Quick changes behind the scenes allowed no time for modesty.

"How've you been, Joe?" Elijah asked.

The boy regained some of his composure. "I'm good," he said, picking the trousers off the floor. "How was *Top Cook*? Did you win?"

"Top secret," he answered with a wink.

"Please, tell me you beat that awful bitch, Keeley Rank?"

Elijah raised both hands. "You know I can't tell you anything. You'll have to wait till it goes out."

"You won," Joe said proudly. "I can tell. Keeley won't have got far. Who'd want to eat anything she made? Vile woman. Her face is enough to put you off. She could never win a challenge like *Top Cook*."

* * * *

"He fancies you." Daniel said, as they left the theater.

"Who?" Elijah asked.

"Joe."

Elijah's brow furrowed. "What? No way. He's just a kid. I'm old enough to be his dad."

"The dad-he'd-like-to-fuck," Daniel said dryly. "I never thought of you as a DILF before."

125

Elijah nudged his arm. "Stop it."

It felt good to joke. Daniel had had little to laugh about today. But now Elijah was here, things would get better.

Elijah waited while he dealt with the crowd at the stage door. The police had yet to release Christian's identity to the press and the people outside were totally unaware of Daniel's connection to the murder on the beach. He signed the usual round of programs and posed for selfies, before climbing into the back of the car with Elijah. They went straight to the hotel.

He couldn't wait to get him alone, behind closed doors.

Elijah's return had had an acute influence on his libido.

Daniel wrapped his arms around him as soon as they entered the suite. He couldn't wait. He needed that close contact. His hands moved to the curve of Elijah's spine and he pressed his forehead to his. They stood in silence for a moment. It was enough — the quiet and the stillness.

"Are you okay?" Elijah asked softly.

"Yes," Daniel answered, then, "No. But I'm better now you're here."

"Are you ready to talk?"

It was one of things Daniel loved about him. Elijah knew how far to go and when to step back. He wouldn't pressure him. He'd wait till he was ready.

"Not yet," Daniel said. "Not until I process it for myself. I'm not sure what I even want to say."

Elijah brushed his lips against his cheek, grazing Daniel's face with his stubble. "Whenever you're ready, I'll listen. You know that."

Daniel moved his hands to Elijah's arse and pulled his hips tight against his own, letting him feel the hardness of his cock through their clothes. The sudden need for him was overwhelming. Elijah murmured appreciatively and thrust his fingers through Daniel's hair, turning his head to face him.

Breathing hot against his face, Elijah moved his lips over Daniel's, teasing him, holding back from the kiss.

In that moment, there was only one thing Daniel wanted.

"Fuck me," he said, breathing heavily. "Fuck me now."

Elijah's hands tightened on his arse, digging deep into mounds of flesh and muscle. "That what you want?" he teased, squeezing harder.

Daniel's cock twitched. He wanted it all right, as badly as he'd ever wanted anything. He grabbed the hem of Elijah's T-shirt and pulled it over his shoulders. Now his hands caressed bare flesh. Daniel sank his head to Elijah's chest and inhaled the scent of his hair, the musk of his skin. He moved his lips toward the hard, swollen nub of Elijah's right nipple. Daniel sucked the tip, then teased with a featherlight touch of his tongue.

Elijah pulled him upright and manhandled him toward the sofa, tugging at his clothes. Daniel's shirt fell first, then Elijah tore into his trousers and yanked them to mid-thigh, together with his underpants. He pushed Daniel onto the sofa and raised his legs to pull off his shorts and trousers.

Daniel surrendered entirely, lifting his knees into his chest to give Elijah unhindered access to his arse. This was what he wanted. To be stripped bare, physically and emotionally. Elijah was the only one who could make him forget what had happened today. For a few minutes, or an hour, nothing else would matter. Just two bodies with a hard desire for each other.

Elijah got on the floor, taking Daniel's hips in both hands, and buried his face in his arse. It was his turn to tease. His tongue skittered around the opening, wet and wonderful.

"Oh, God," Daniel gasped, pulling his knees in tighter. It drove him crazy.

His head was a mess. A turmoil of fractured images flashed through his mind. He saw the boys of Overload in their younger days, and Christian, the eighteen-year-old he'd known back then and the man he'd met last night. The man who was dead today. He needed Elijah to take him forcefully and remind him of where he was. To rid him of the past and his anxiety about the future, to root him here, in the present, just the two of them.

Elijah retrieved a sachet of lube from his discarded jacket and ditched the rest of his clothes. Daniel readied himself on the sofa, hitching his butt to the edge, watching Elijah as he spread the lube over the length of his cock. His palm squelched as he coated his thick, swollen member. Daniel groaned as Elijah pushed his fingers into his arse, preparing the way.

"Don't hold back," Daniel cried.

Elijah gave him exactly what he wanted, easing inside until his hips pressed tight against his upturned butt. Daniel felt raw, vulnerable, exposed, desperately in need of physical relief. He wrapped his legs around Elijah's waist, locking him inside, owning every inch of him. They fucked hard, like animals locked in a love fight. Daniel cried out. He was rarely this vocal but as they reached a long, drawn-out climax, Daniel roared his relief.

"You needed that," Elijah said, lying on top, holding his head in his hands.

Daniel couldn't speak. Didn't have to. Their bodies said enough.

When Elijah eventually withdrew, he left an emptiness behind. Daniel gazed at the ceiling, willing that hollowness to occupy his whole body, to wipe his mind of angst.

While Elijah was in the bathroom, Daniel rolled over to check his phone. The voicemail alert flashed as he picked it up. Ben. He listened carefully.

"Hi, Dan. Just checking in. I caught up with Lars an hour ago. He's coping pretty well, considering. Though I don't think it's hit him yet. It can't have. He IDed Christian's body earlier. The cops arranged for him to see a doctor and they've given him something to sleep. He's going home tomorrow but I think he'd like to see you, if you're around before he goes. I'll call you in the morning to make plans. Good night, mate. Take care."

Daniel wiped away a silent tear. *Poor Lars.* When he woke that morning, he must have believed his life was perfect. A loving husband and a young family. That had all been torn apart.

For what? Daniel wondered if they would ever know.

He already had suspicions about certain things. Things that couldn't be true.

Elijah took him to bed and held him beneath the covers. Outside, the rush of sea against the shore sounded so peaceful. Listening to it in the dark, he found it hard to believe anything so terrible could have happened out there. But it had, less than twenty-four hours earlier.

"I'm going to see Christian's husband in the morning," Daniel said, rolling over to rest his head on Elijah's shoulder.

"Can I come?" Elijah asked, rubbing his face against the top of Daniel's head.

"I'd like it if you did."

"What was Christian like?"

Daniel sighed. "A nice guy. He was the big brother of the band. The sensible one who kept things moving. Who got us to the airports on time and made sure we went to bed when we had an early start the next day. I'm not surprised he adopted children. He'd make a fantastic dad."

The tears came again. Silent and profound, they rolled across his cheeks, onto Elijah's shoulder. He didn't try to stop them.

He was safe.

Elijah quietly embraced him as grief took its course.

Chapter Eleven

In the early hours of Wednesday morning, a man walked into an all-night café in a backstreet on the south side of town. None of the customers paid him much attention. They were either drunk or had enough concerns of their own. But the man was careful and wore one of the disguises he adopted around town. He had to be cautious at all times.

He approached the counter with his shoulders slouched and his head down. He wore a baseball cap pulled low over his forehead and large, clear-lensed glasses. In grubby jogging pants and a scruffy hoodie, he looked perfectly at home in the greasy-spoon café.

"What can I get you, love?" The woman behind the counter looked to be in her late sixties and tired. Very tired. She had faded tattoos on both of her forearms and her blue tabard was stained with sauce and gravy.

"Bacon and egg roll," he answered in an affected cockney accent. "And a pot of tea."

The waitress threw a tea bag into a stainless-steel pot and filled it with scalding water. A wall-mounted TV above the counter showed an all-night casino show. The woman put the teapot on a small tray with a jug of milk and a mug. "There's sugar on the tables, love. I'll bring your sandwich over when it's done. Four pound thirty, please."

He paid her in loose change and took his tray to a table in the corner, as far as he could get from the other customers.

Unable to sleep, Sonny Rock had had to get out of his shithole flat. The cloying smell of damp and mold infused everything in the rotten place. He could still smell it here, despite the heavy atmosphere of grease. Sonny had enough self-awareness to know that he'd go crazy if he stayed in all night. The flat remined him of prison.

It was a dump, but it suited his purpose. No one paid him any attention. No one would notice when he moved on and if the cops came sniffing around, no one would have seen a thing. It was easy to get lost among the druggies, drunks and no-hopers in the neighborhood.

Sonny spooned two mounds of sugar into a mug and poured the tea. He needed time to think. A clear head, away from the oppressive environment of the flat. Things were moving faster than he'd planned. Nothing he couldn't handle, but it was essential to keep his focus. Stay fixed on his target and be aware of what was happening at all times.

Earlier in the evening, he'd attended the performance of *Lady Lynda* at the Winter Gardens. He'd bought tickets for every show this week. It was unlikely he would attend them all, but he'd prepared just the same.

Tonight, for insistence, he couldn't have missed that.

Sonny wasn't surprised to see that Daniel Blake had performed.

He was a professional. The death of an old boyfriend wouldn't keep him from the stage. Or maybe Christian hadn't meant that much to him after all.

Sonny noticed a newspaper at the next table. It was a well-read, food-stained evening edition of the local rag. He snatched it over. The body on the beach filled the whole of the front page, as rightly it should. They had yet to reveal the identity of the victim. That would come with the morning papers.

"Terrible business, isn't it?" The waitress arrived, putting his sandwich in front of him. "I've heard all sorts of stories since I came in tonight. They say he had his heart cut out. Can you imagine? Who'd do such a thing? There are some sick minds out there, I'll say. The killer might have walked through that door for all I know. We get all sorts in here. Just last year, we had a guy who smashed his wife's brains in, then came here for a full English afterward. Calm as you like, he was."

Sonny ignored her and squirted ketchup on his sandwich. The waitress, realizing she didn't have much of an audience, moved back to the counter.

He bit into the roll, dripping egg yolk and sauce across the plate.

Sonny hadn't meant to kill Christian Gates. The plan had been to deal with Daniel first. That was what had brought him to Blackpool. It was pure chance that the other two had shown up. Sonny couldn't have designed it better. He had seen Ben at the theater last night and thought he looked familiar, but it was only when he'd followed them to Daniel's hotel that he'd been sure.

He hadn't known what he was going do at that point, but it had been too good an opportunity to waste.

Three of his five targets had been in the same place at the same time.

It was a gift from God.

If God was on the side of men like Sonny Rock.

He smiled at the idea.

The murder of Luke Torrens in July had been easy. Like a trial run. The most low-key of the Overload singers, Luke had made the perfect first victim. Just a regular guy with an ordinary life. Sonny had gambled that his death wouldn't make much impact and he had been right. It had barely gained coverage in the Bournemouth press. None of the nationals had touched it. Torrens had been a nobody. Sonny hadn't needed the attention at that stage. Nothing that might alert the others to the danger they were in.

Their time would come, and when it did, they would know about it.

But not until he was ready.

When Christian had left the hotel alone, Sonny had seen a chance and taken it. He'd followed him to the seafront, watched him take the slow walk back to his hotel in the middle of the night with no one else around. Some people were born to be victims. They invited it. Seizing him had been easy. Once on the beach, away from the lights of the promenade, Sonny could do what he liked.

Like cutting out his heart. A spur-of-the-moment decision. Fucked-up, for sure — Christian had still been alive when the knife had gone in — but Sonny had always enjoyed hurting people.

Earlier today, he had driven out of town in another disguise, up onto the moors, where he'd incinerated last night's clothes. He'd even gotten rid of the weapon, tossing it into the sea. There was nothing to tie him to the killing. Let the police look for a connection. They would never find it.

Sonny finished his sandwich and wiped his lips. It was delicious. Sometimes protein and fat were all it took to sort out a muddled head.

It was almost five. The start of another day. He had to consider his next move carefully. Christian's murder had been an improvisation, with no time to do the things he would have liked. To make him suffer before the end. He wouldn't be denied that indulgence again. Daniel and Ben would experience maximum pain before he was done.

They were good-looking bastards. Both of them. Maybe he should cut up their faces. Take off their lips, noses and eyelids.

Sonny adjusted his hard-on beneath the table.

The anticipation of violence was almost as thrilling as the deed.

He finished the tea and left the café, much happier than when he'd arrived. He'd go back to the flat and catch a few hours' sleep before deciding what to do with the day.

As he walked, his mobile rang, an unregistered pay-as-you-go device. The ID of the caller was blank.

"I've just seen the news," a voice said. "This isn't what we agreed. You were supposed to deal with Daniel."

Sonny inhaled the fresh morning air and smiled. "There's been a change of plan," he said. "I think you're going to like it."

Chapter Twelve

After breakfast on Wednesday, Daniel and Elijah took a walk, accompanied at a respectful distance by a plain-clothed police officer.

"I feel like a fraud," Daniel said as they walked along the North Pier. "They must have better things to do than follow me around."

"Take it easy," Elijah said. "It's for your own good. If the cops want to follow you, then let them. Until we know exactly what happened to Christian, I feel better knowing they're looking out for you."

A blustery wind blew in from the Irish Sea. For the first time in weeks, Daniel wore a jacket to go outside. It was a timely reminder that summer had reached an end, with autumn about to strike. Daniel raised his chin to the wind and enjoyed the sensations as it tore through his hair. It was difficult to believe on a morning such as this that there was anything wrong in the world. Especially with Elijah beside him.

He didn't have to think too hard to know the opposite was true.

He'd needed to get away from the hotel and the gossipy speculation he heard in the public areas. The morning headlines had carried the identity of the body on the beach. As yet, no one had made the connection between Christian and Overload, but they would, and soon., before the morning was out. Daniel had to make the most of these moments of calm before the storm struck.

This morning, while Elijah was in the shower, he'd tried to find out what had happened to Luke Torrens. There wasn't much to go on. Most of the media outlets that had reported his death carried the same few facts — he had been found dead in his shop soon after opening one morning. The police were treating his death as a bungled robbery and had yet make an arrest.

Daniel doubted they would.

Surely it was coincidence. There was nothing to tie the two murders, apart from the connection the victims had as teenagers. However Daniel tried to rationalize it, that undeniable fact remained.

Can the same person be responsible for both of their deaths? No, it's too much of a stretch.

They reached the end of the pier. Sandy-colored waves washed around the structure beneath them as the tide came in. Daniel gripped the railing and leaned into the wind.

"I still love the sea," he said.

Elijah stood behind him with his hands on his waist and rested his chin on Daniel's shoulder. "Me too. There's no reason not to. It isn't responsible for what happened on the *Anthem*. Human failing was."

Daniel closed his eyes and surrendered to the elements, to the man behind him. He'd needed no one until now. Before Elijah, he'd always done his own thing — been independent since he'd been sixteen years old. He'd traveled the world by himself. How would he handle the situation now if he was still alone?

Thankfully, he didn't have to know. He wasn't alone. They were in this together.

Returning to the hotel, they met Ben in the lobby. Daniel introduced him to Elijah and watched as they shook hands then hugged like old friends.

"It's good to meet you," Elijah said. "I wish the circumstances had been better."

"Ain't that the truth?" Ben replied, patting his back before breaking apart.

Ben looked to be bearing the strain well. His clothes were clean and he had trimmed his beard. He even raised a smile for Elijah, flashing his famous dimples, but around his eyes, the tension showed.

"How are you feeling?" Daniel asked.

"I won't lie. I've been better."

"Any more news?" Elijah asked.

"No. But I've got a friendly policeman trailing me around, so I guess they think one of us will be next."

"Do you believe that?" Daniel asked.

Ben shrugged. "Hardly seem likely, does it? But neither did Christian's murder."

They shared a car to The Imperial Hotel, where Ben had arranged a room for Lars. Daniel's pulse quickened on the short drive along the seafront, past the spot where Christian had been killed. Yellow crime tape was strung across the railings of the promenade and fluttered ominously in the wind.

"Has Lars seen this?" His throat was tight. He tried hard to swallow.

Ben nodded grimly. "The cops brought him down last night. He insisted on seeing where it happened."

"Shit," Elijah gasped.

Tears pricked at Daniel's eyes. He fought them back. *Be strong*, he told himself. *No tears in public. Not today.*

"Press," Elijah warned as they pulled up into the car park.

A small local news crew, just one van, a cameraman and a reporter, were shooting a link in front of the hotel. A handful of people had gathered to watch the filming.

Elijah told the driver to get them as close to the door as possible. As they came to a halt, Daniel jumped out and rushed into the foyer before the reporters could spot him. The chances of getting out unseen were miniscule. Once someone in the hotel realized he was visiting Christian's husband, they'd tip off the press or post it on social media. Either way, the Overload connection would be public knowledge soon.

What does it matter? Your friend is dead. Who cares about you? He was angry. Why did he care about what they reported? It was hardly important. He was about to meet a man who'd lost the love of his life, his soulmate. What did a little heat from the press matter?

They went up to a room on the third floor. A plump, middle-aged man in a checked shirt and maroon chinos answered the door. "Hello, I'm Rudy," he said, shaking hands. "I work with Lars. I was with him when he got the news and drove up here with him."

"How is he this morning?" Ben asked quietly.

"Coping," Rudy answered, barely above a whisper. "Come on in."

They followed him to the sitting room. There were a couple of carrier bags on the coffee table, filled with bottles of water and snacks.

"We didn't have time for overnight bags," Rudy explained. "I got what I could from the convenience store on the corner."

A noise from the bedroom made Daniel turn. A tall, haunted-looking man wearing suit trousers and an open-necked shirt came out.

Lars Kristoffersen looked a lot like Christian. They were reflections of each other, like brothers. He had the same short blond hair — *they probably go to the same barber*, Daniel thought — and the same blue eyes. But today, his eyes were raw. It would be a long time before they sparkled again.

"I'm so sorry," Daniel said, going to him.

"Thanks for coming," Lars replied, taking his hand. "It means a lot to know you care."

"I do. Oh, God, I do. If there's anything you need, or anything you want, you only have to say."

"I want to take Christian home," he said quietly.

"Of course."

"The police won't tell us when they'll release the bod...Christian. When they'll release Christian," Rudy said. He looked mortified, realizing what he'd said.

"It's an investigation," Ben said. "I know you want him back, but you want them to be thorough too. So they can catch the bastard who did it."

Lars nodded. "Let's sit."

He walked as if he were in a trance — a sleepwalker, moving by instinct, with no real awareness of where he is. Daniel kept a hand on his elbow and guided him to the sofa.

"I haven't told the kids," Lars said at last. "I'll speak to them tonight. When we get home."

"There's no rush," Rudy told him.

"They have to know," Lars insisted. "Christian's name is on the news now. They're too young to notice that, but someone will tell them if I don't. It has to come from me."

"Of course," Daniel said.

Lars raised his eyes to look at him. "I wish we'd met before. Christian has always spoken with huge affection of his time in the band. He's got one of your record covers framed in his study. They were happy days for him."

Daniel swallowed with difficulty. He couldn't speak—he was too close to losing it.

"We should have staged a reunion," Ben said.

"Yes," Lars answered. "There's lot of things Christian should have done. It's too late for any of them now."

* * * *

"Jesus, that poor guy," Elijah said. "He's in agony."

"He's in hell," Daniel stated softly.

They were in a taxi back to The Majestic, just the two of them. Ben wanted to wait behind and see Lars off. Daniel also wanted to stay, but he had a matinee this afternoon and was required at the theater by two.

Reporters had gathered at the hotel when they left, and the concierge had let them out of a back door to the waiting taxi to avoid them. But they would be there at the theater this afternoon, waiting for their opportunity at the stage door.

Daniel reached across the back seat for Elijah's hand. He held it and squeezed.

"Let's call on Max," Elijah said when they arrived at the hotel. "It's been ages since I saw her."

They went straight to her room.

"Come in," she said enthusiastically as she answered the door. She threw her arms around Elijah's neck and stood on tiptoes to kiss him. "Welcome back, darling. It's been a terrible couple of days, but things will be better now you're here."

"We've just come from seeing Ben and Lars," Daniel said, explaining what had gone down at The Imperial.

"Any news from the cops?" Max asked, leading them into the living room. Her iPad lay face-up on the coffee table. Daniel recognized one of the old Overload songs playing on YouTube.

"Nothing," he announced. "What are you watching?"

Max picked up the tablet and shut it down. "I've been watching some of your old videos. It sounds like stalking, but I just wanted to remind myself of what you guys were like. My God, you were babies."

"It was a long time ago," Daniel said.

"How is Ben holding up?" she asked.

"He seems okay." In truth, Daniel didn't have a clue how he was coping. They hadn't seen each other in so long. Ben appeared to be dealing well, but how would Daniel know if he wasn't? He used to get on with Ben but had always been closer to Christian. "You like him, don't you?"

Max got up and crossed to the window. "Oh, I don't know. Yes, of course, I like him, but we've just met. And he's so much younger than I me. It's kind of weird."

"Age means nothing," Elijah said.

"That's easy for you to say. But I'm fifty-four. I could have given birth to the whole band."

"Oh, come off it. That doesn't mean a thing. No one gives a shit about age. Not these days. Ben's not a boy anymore. He's a man. When are you seeing him again?" Daniel asked.

"Soon, I hope. But he's got a lot going on right now. Maybe he won't have time for an old woman like me."

"Give it rest," Daniel said. "If he likes you, and I'm sure he does, he'll make time."

* * * *

As they returned to Daniel's suite, Elijah took hold of him.

"I have to get ready for the theater," Daniel said.

Elijah pulled him close, chest against chest. He pressed his lips against Daniel's neck. "The theater can wait," Elijah said softly. "First I want to know how *you* are. Really. How are you feeling?"

With a long exhalation, Daniel relaxed into Elijah's arms and abandoned himself. "I'm all right."

"Seriously?"

"It's true. I promise. I'm fine. Better today than I was yesterday."

Elijah squeezed him and turned his head to kiss him on the mouth. Daniel wasn't lying. He was in a better place today than he'd been last night. Thanks to Elijah. Now he was here, things were more bearable. In the sober light of day, the idea that someone wanted to kill him seemed impossible. Ridiculous.

"Let's go away," Daniel said, moving his hands to Elijah's butt, his favorite place. "We've talked about a holiday, let's do it. When the show wraps up on Saturday, let's take off right away. The same night."

"Are you sure?" Elijah asked softly. "Don't you want to be here for the funeral? It'll likely be sometime next week."

Daniel deflated. He hadn't thought of that. "Shit, you're right. What kind of friend am I? Planning a holiday when Christian is barely cold. That's sick."

Elijah hugged him tighter. "Go easy on yourself. We can still do it. We don't have to go far. There are plenty of remote places in the UK, far from anywhere. The Scottish Highlands, the Welsh valleys, the Northumberland coast. I'll look into it and find somewhere to escape to. We'll still be around when they set a funeral date."

Daniel blinked and two tears squeezed from his eyes. Elijah caught them, brushing them dry with his thumbs. "Thank you," Daniel whispered.

Elijah kissed him on the mouth. "I'm here. You don't have to face any of this alone."

Daniel put his head on Elijah's shoulder and let it rest. He'd never needed or appreciated anyone as much as he did in that moment.

Chapter Thirteen

The strain of the last two days took nothing away from Daniel's performance. From his seat, midway in the stalls, Elijah saw none of the personal crisis in his delivery that afternoon. Daniel immersed himself in the character and gave the matinee audience the show they had paid for. He couldn't decide whether that was a good thing or not. While the show offered Daniel a distraction from events around him, he didn't know how healthy that would be in the long run. However rough things got, it was better to face the truth than hide from it.

Elijah tried not to dwell on the idea. He couldn't put himself in Daniel's place. He didn't know what it was like to lead a major show. Daniel's name blazed on posters all over town, on the sides of trams and buses. There were only a few performances left. By Saturday it would all be over. Whatever techniques Daniel had to employ to get through the week, Elijah would support him, even if that meant ignoring the danger he might be in. Elijah had his back. Daniel could focus on the show and he'd make sure nothing happened to him.

Elijah had a foreboding sense of déjà vu. It had struck the minute he got the call about Christian and had only deepened since his arrival in Blackpool. He couldn't ignore it. What had happened to Daniel on the *Anthem*, linked directly to his time in Overload. It wasn't over. But whatever way he looked at it, Elijah couldn't make out what the connection might be.

Oliver had killed himself, leaping into a furious oceanic storm. Suicide — pure and simple. Christian and Luke had been murdered in unrelated circumstances. *Seemingly* unrelated. They were connected all right. Elijah felt certain.

He had no option but to look after Daniel until the cops figured out what it was.

The curtain came down on act one and the audience responded appreciatively. As the house lights came up, Elijah turned to Ben in the next seat.

"That went well, don't you think?"

Ben nodded. "One hundred percent. I almost forgot my own worries for a little while."

He suspected Ben's smile, like Daniel's, masked a muddle of anger, grief and anxiety. They both put on a good front.

"Feel like a drink?" Elijah asked. "There's time before the second act, if we're quick."

"Good call," Ben answered, getting to his feet.

They followed the crowd out of the opera house into the main concourse of the Winter Gardens. Amid the shuffling patrons, he caught snatches of conversation.

"Isn't he amazing? You wouldn't know anything was wrong."

"Simply superb. I don't know how he does it."

"He deserves an award. Putting on a performance like that after everything he's been through. I've not seen anyone like him."

So, Elijah thought, *the word is out*. He shouldn't be surprised. Christian wasn't just another tourist coming to an untimely end during the boozy summer season. *Lady Lynda* was the hottest ticket in town and the dead man had a connection to the star. That wasn't just local news. It was national. There'd be a horde of reporters at the stage door by the end of the day.

He'd shield Daniel from the worst of it, but they'd have to get on with it. They had enough experience of dealing with the press. Reporters had been a constant factor in their lives since they'd met. Just a few more days and they could leave it all behind.

He headed into the bar with Ben.

"What'll you have?" Ben asked.

"A beer," he answered.

The bar was crowded, with most of the tables already taken. Elijah found a space to stand against one of the dark-paneled posts. It also allowed him to stay out of sight of the main crush. Several people had already recognized him, nodding and pointing enthusiastically in his direction. He always had time for people who wanted to hello, but not today.

He observed Ben at the bar, already getting served. His stature and good looks meant he'd never had to wait long. He didn't know much about Ben, or any of Daniel's band mates. Overload wasn't a subject Daniel liked to talk about and Elijah didn't push it. Daniel would open up when he was ready. They didn't even have any of their old CDs at home. Elijah had done his own research and knew the basics. The guys had had a brief moment in the spotlight when they were young, racking up a handful of minor hits without making it big. They had been dropped by their record label and management after one album. The boys had gone their separate ways and hadn't stayed in touch.

Like most manufactured boy bands, the guys had had their own characters within the group. Daniel had been the youngest and naturally the baby. The most innocent-looking of the five, he'd appealed to the pre-pubescent music fan. Blond and healthy, Christian had been the good-looking boy-next-door. Luke Torrens, with an eyebrow piercing and multiple tattoos, had played the pseudo-bad boy. David Kharsa had been the dark and moody one, while Ben, with his infectious smile and dimples, was the cheeky one. Elijah had watched archived interviews with the band from their heyday and they always stayed in character, never deviating from type.

Like Daniel, Ben had gotten better with age. The weathering of time had made his face less pretty, more interesting — sexier — than before. Elijah noticed the way people at the bar were looking at him. Both men and women checked him out with undisguised lust. Their eyes pursued him as he returned with two bottles of beer.

"Cheers," he said, handing Elijah a bottle.

"Cheers." They clinked bottle necks before drinking. Elijah swallowed the cold brew appreciatively. "I needed that."

Ben sighed. "I could use something stronger, to tell the truth, but beer will do for now."

Elijah nodded. "I know what you mean. Tough week, but you've both handled it brilliantly. I'm here for Daniel, but I want you to know that I'm here for you too. If there's anything you want, or anything I can do, just say it."

"Thanks, man, I appreciate it. Right now, I don't know what I want. A tiny part of me wants to run. Just take off and never look back."

"I wouldn't blame you if you did."

He shook his head. "A bigger part of me wants to stay. Needs to stay. I don't know why, but I feel my place is here. With Max. With Daniel."

"They appreciate it, I'm certain."

Ben sipped his beer thoughtfully and said, "You know, you two make a perfect couple. I used to think that, seeing you in magazines and newspapers, but when I saw the pair of you this morning, together, I realized how true it is. You're like two halves that make a whole."

"I feel the same," Elijah admitted. "I have done since I met him."

"Good. I'm glad to see him happy. He deserves it more than anyone." He swallowed and suddenly seemed ill at ease, struggling with what he wanted to say. "Just...just take care of him, man. Christian was happy too, so very happy. His life was perfect and now it's over."

Elijah put down his beer and stepped closer. People were watching but he didn't care. *Let them look*. He put his arm around Ben's shoulder and felt the tension in his muscles. "Let's look out for each other, eh? I don't want anything bad happening to anyone else. There's been enough shit already. Let's make things better."

"Thanks," he drawled. "And sorry. I guess...this is getting to me. I'm not usually like this. Such a mess. I've always done my own thing and pleased myself. Now, I just can't shake the feeling that someone is controlling me instead."

"What do you mean?"

"Someone is watching us. It's the only explanation. They watched and waited till Christian was alone."

So, Elijah wasn't alone in his suspicion. "You don't think it was a coincidence then? First Luke, and now Christian."

Ben's lips drew back into a sneer. "Not a fucking chance. To the cops, it doesn't look like the two are connected, but I don't buy that. Oliver, Luke, Christian — who'll be next? It's like we're characters in a whodunit. *And Then There Were None*. Something is seriously wrong. This is all part of a bigger picture. Some huge, fucked-up picture. And we're right in the middle of it."

* * * *

They returned to their seats for the second half of the show. Although Daniel and the rest of the cast performed to the same standard as before, Elijah struggled to engage with the story. Talking to Ben had only confirmed what he already feared. If it were true, if they weren't being paranoid, whoever had murdered Luke had also murdered Christian, and that person was likely to be in Blackpool right now. Why wouldn't they be? If destroying Overload was the goal, then two of the targets were right there waiting.

Daniel was lying full length on the sofa in his dressing room when Elijah entered after the show. His eyes opened.

"Hey," Elijah spoke quietly. "Want me to leave you in peace?"

Daniel shook his head. "Just resting my eyes for a minute, that's all." He'd taken off his stage clothes. All he wore was a pair of white boxer-briefs and dark socks. His body was perfect. Eight shows a week, all that singing and dancing, had made him leaner and harder. The hair had grown back across his chest and belly, making the scars almost invisible. Elijah, knowing where they were, still had to look for them.

"What happened to the guy guarding your door?" Elijah asked, pushing the bolt into place behind him. "There's nobody out there."

"His name is Rory," Daniel said. "I told him to take a break."

"Is that wise?"

"It seems unnecessary, him being there. I'm in a theater full of people. I don't think anything could happened here."

"Better safe than sorry, Daniel. If the theater can spare this guy to look out for you, you should take advantage."

Daniel smiled. "I don't need to take advantage of Rory. I've got you for that."

He's deflecting again. Elijah didn't push it. He would speak to Rory himself. Tell him to stick close to Daniel, no matter what he told him to do.

"That was another great show," Elijah said. "You raised the roof."

"I do my best." He rose onto one elbow. "What are people saying? I take it the news about Christian has spread."

"Nothing much. Everything I heard was very supportive. Those people in the audience are rooting for you. They've got your back."

He didn't tell him about the commotion at the stage door. Elijah had looked out after the show to see what was going on. The reporters who'd been hanging around the hotel that morning had relocated to the theater. Only there were more of them. It wasn't just a local story, the nationals were on to it. TV and print. They all wanted a piece.

Daniel didn't need to know that yet.

The matinee crowd didn't expect autographs or selfies, so Daniel had no reason to go out there. In less than two hours, he had to do the show all over again. Better that he stay here and save his energy.

"Have you eaten?" Elijah asked.

"I've got a snack to have in a little while. How about you?"

"I'll get something during the second show."

"How about booking us that holiday?"

"I'm on it." He smiled.

Daniel pushed up into a sitting position. His hair stuck up where he'd been lying. The disheveled look suited him. Everything suited him. "Come here," he said, opening his arms.

His hair wasn't the only thing sticking up. The protrusion in his pants was unmissable.

Elijah sat beside him. "What's this?" he asked, putting his hand on the bulge, squeezing its hardness.

"Something that needs taking care of," he answered, pushing against Elijah's palm. "I don't want people saying I'm stiff onstage."

Elijah chuckled. It might be another of Daniel's deflections, but he would not complain. He slid from the sofa to the floor, getting on his knees in front of Daniel. Daniel's thighs were muscular, like a dancer's. Elijah put his hands on their hairy bulk and spread them wide, moving his head to Daniel's groin. He could feel the heat of Daniel's cock and could smell it. The white cotton of his boxer briefs molded to the stiff contours of his dick. Elijah could even make out the outline of veins. Where the head lay, the fabric was already dark and damp.

He slid a hand inside the right leg, pulling the briefs aside to withdraw the hard length of Daniel's dick. He slipped the other hand inside to ease Daniel's balls the same way. Elijah palmed the sac and squeezed gently. Just a little pressure.

Daniel groaned encouragement.

Opening his mouth, Elijah drew the sticky head inside, giving Daniel exactly what he needed.

* * * *

Joe Elliott hovered at the door of Daniel's dressing room with his ear to the wood. *They're definitely doing it.* The guttural, animalistic groans that issued from inside were unmistakable. Sex. The temptation to knock and quickly enter was damn near irresistible. To walk in and see them at it — naked and screwing. Lord, just a glimpse of that would be enough.

But the door was probably locked. Daniel and Elijah were not a pair of tawdry exhibitionists. If they were getting down to it, they wouldn't take any chances. And how sad would he look, rattling a locked door? Beyond desperate.

But he was desperate. In three more days, the show would be over. Then what? Then nothing. He wouldn't see either of them again.

A painful knot tightened in his chest. *It's my heart constricting for Elijah. Slowly killing me for a man I can't have. I just know it.*

Joe's feelings for him grew stronger and more intense every day. He was all Joe could think about. Kissing that mouth, stroking that hair, wrapping his lips around that dick. Oh, God, he wanted him badly. It hurt all over.

Listening to them now didn't make it any better. It made it worse.

"Oh, yes," Daniel cried from the other side of the door. "Let me in, I've missed you so much."

Daniel is fucking Elijah. Joe had always assumed Daniel would be a total bottom and Elijah a top. Not so. From the sound of this they were both entirely versatile. Joe's brain struggled to cope with the ball of emotions — excitement, jealousy, confusion. He formed a picture of what was going down beyond the door. Of Elijah bent over the dressing table with his trousers around his ankles, while Daniel pounded him from behind.

Joe's cock swelled in his underwear. Now he'd thought about it, Elijah giving up his arse was a sweet idea. Not that he wanted to plunder Elijah's butt himself. Joe was one hundred percent bottom. He wanted Elijah deep in his own hole, screwing him hard and fast, then slow and thorough. The fantasy had sustained him through many hot and sticky nights this summer. Daddy Elijah reaming him inside and out.

Time was running out if Joe wanted to make that dream a reality.

He needed a plan of seduction. And fast.

Chapter Fourteen

The rest of the week passed with little incident. If it wasn't for the police officers assigned to watch him, Daniel could almost believe life had returned to normal. DI Ritson visited him at the hotel on Thursday morning with little to report.

"There have been no further developments in the case," the inspector stated gravely.

Daniel's hands tightened in his lap. The cops claimed to have nothing. He didn't believe it. "I heard someone might have seen Christian walking toward the beach on Monday night," Daniel informed him.

"Where did you hear that?" Ritson asked haughtily.

"The theater. If you want to know anything, ask the backstage crew. They always know what's going on. My dresser told me last night. A drag queen from one of the show bars saw someone who looked like Christian while they were walking home from work. Have you interviewed them?"

Ritson nodded. "We have."

"And did they see anything?" Daniel found Ritson's laid-back tone infuriating. It sounded like he was running an investigation for a missing cat, not a dead man.

"Nothing we didn't already know. The witness places Christian close to the beach at the time of death. But they saw no one else in the area and heard nothing."

"Damn."

"I understand your frustration," Ritson said. "But we're giving this investigation maximum resources. We'll catch who did this."

Daniel kept his mouth shut. Arguing with the police wouldn't achieve anything. Besides, he was angry with himself, not them. If he'd been more aware of what went on around him, less self-obsessed and insular, he might have picked up on the danger they were in. More than anyone, he should have been alert to it. Had he learned nothing from the *Anthem*?

How many more people will die because of me?

Daniel spent the little time he had researching what had happened to Luke Torrens in Bournemouth. He had to be careful. He didn't want Elijah to find out and think he was dwelling on the morbid details. He would only worry.

Information about Luke's murder was scant. A handful of local news outlets reported the same few details. A robbery gone wrong. No suspects. No arrests.

No hope.

More interesting were the facts he learned about Luke himself. Like the rest of the boys, Daniel had lost touch with him after the band collapsed. Luke had been living in Bournemouth for most of that time. He'd married a local girl, had two kids and started his own business. Someone had amended his Facebook page to become a tribute. Hundreds of people had left messages of condolence.

Daniel repeatedly returned to the page, checking his phone in the quiet moments he had to himself, studying the photos Luke had uploaded to his timeline. They provided a visual narrative for the last decade of his life. Luke had probably changed the most out of the Overload boys. He had filled out in the years since his wedding, settling into a life of contentment and family. He'd lost most of his hair by the time he was thirty and his face had the ruddy, sunburned appearance of a man who spent his weekends catching the sun and the surf.

The last picture had been uploaded the week before he died. It showed Luke on the beach, in a wetsuit with his boys, soaking wet and smiling. It was the photo that brought Daniel the most comfort, knowing Luke enjoyed a happy, fulfilled life.

Until someone had decided to end it.

Daniel had to face the hard reality that, however good things appeared to be, death was never far away.

* * * *

On Thursday night, he received a visitor after the show.

He was in the dressing room with Joe, pulling on his own clothes before heading home, when there was a sudden knock at the door and it opened without delay.

"Surprise, darling," a familiar voice announced broadly.

Terry St. King stood in the doorway with his arms held wide. He wore a white tuxedo with a silver tie. His thin hair, as white as the suit, had been blown and teased into a semi-transparent crown. From the entrance, his heavy cologne filled the room.

"Terry. Oh, my God."

Daniel rushed across the room to embrace him. Beneath the suit, Terry felt like a fragile bird in his arms. Terry held him close, rubbing his hands reassuringly across his shoulders.

"I didn't know you were coming," Daniel said.

"Didn't want to steal your thunder, darling." Terry held him at arm's length, getting a good look at him. "Not that I ever could. You were wonderful. Simply the best."

"Would you have said that about me this time last year?" Daniel teased.

"God, no," Terry cried. "You were an annoying little shit. Or so I thought. Is that champagne, darling? I'm rather parched."

"Help yourself." Daniel laughed.

Terry's attitude had mellowed since they had first met on the *Anthem,* when Terry had made no secret of the fact he couldn't stand him. But that had quickly changed. If not for Terry, Daniel wouldn't have been here at all. He owed Terry St. King his life.

Terry might have softened toward Daniel, but he had a diva reputation to maintain. "You, boy," he said and snapped bejeweled fingers at Joe. "Be a sweetie and pour me a glass of the fizzy stuff. There's a good lad."

Joe stared disconcertedly between Daniel and Terry, before grabbing a fresh glass and pouring the fizz.

A small woman in her early sixties hovered nervously in the doorway. She wore a brown suit that had seen better days and looked tight across the bust and hips, and narrow-framed glasses.

"Don't stand there on ceremony," Terry said grandly, waving her in. "This is Muriel. She's my PA, secretary, traveling companion and a host of other things besides."

Muriel smiled and nodded apologetically. Daniel sat on the sofa and indicated for her to join him. Joe poured a second glass and handed it to her.

"This is Joe," Daniel said. "He's been taking care of me while I've been working here."

"Oh, so he comes with the room," Terry said archly. "I thought for an awful moment that you'd traded the lovely Elijah in for a younger model."

Joe blushed.

"Joe's a godsend, but I don't intend trading Elijah in for anyone. Not ever," Daniel said.

"I should think not."

Terry looked a lot thinner than when Daniel had seen him last. Even then he'd had little weight to spare. There were signs he'd had work done too. An inexpressive quality to his brow, a smoothness to his top lip, the crepey smoker's lines from around his mouth had disappeared. His teeth could also be new. They looked bigger than ever, though that could be due to the weight loss.

Terry's career had received an unexpected boost when he'd emerged as the man who saved Daniel's life. No longer confined to the lounges of cruise ships, his act was in huge demand. Only a couple of weeks back, while Daniel was channel surfing, he'd come across Terry on some daytime antiques show, one of four celebrities hunting for bargains in a car boot sale.

"What are you up to now?" Daniel asked.

"Oh, this and that," he said. "You know what it's like. TV, theater, cabaret, everyone wants a slice."

"Terry has just completed a twenty-date UK tour," Muriel added. "And we're gearing up for the release of his autobiography in November."

"Wow," Daniel said. "That's amazing. I can't wait to read it."

"I haven't yet read it myself." Terry laughed. "I sat down with a gorgeous little ghost writer earlier this year and told her the whole story. She's written the book. I've only seen bits and pieces so far, but it's looking rather marvelous."

"Too busy to write your own book?" Daniel teased.

"I'm too busy to wipe my arse some days. It's a nightmare."

Daniel laughed. Terry loved it. His age was a deep secret. Some people said he was seventy, others that he was nearer eighty, but whatever the truth, Terry had finally achieved the level of celebrity he believed he deserved.

"I hope you're having a book launch. Send me an invitation," Daniel said.

"I will. I want you there. And Elijah, of course. We all deserve a good party."

"I won't argue about that. How long are you in Blackpool for? We're having a wrap party on Saturday. You should come. Elijah will be pissed he missed you tonight."

Terry's smile finally faded. "I'd love to but have to move on first thing. I've got a gig in Scotland tomorrow night. To be honest, I should be there now. They had some promotional work lined up for me in the morning. But when I read about your friend in the papers this week, I had to come and see you. Daniel, I'm so sorry. It's fucking awful."

Daniel bit his upper lip. A rush of emotion threatened to overtake him, but he would not cry.

"I saw the cops at the stage door," Terry continued. "So, that's a good thing, at least. They're looking after you."

"I haven't gotten used to them," Daniel admitted.

Terry nodded. "You don't think…this has anything to do with…that little shit who shall not be named?"

Daniel shrugged. "On one hand I can't see how it could. And on the other, I can't shake the feeling that it must do."

"Shit." Terry put down his glass and came to Daniel. He knelt on the floor, placing both hands on his knees. "Answer me honestly. Are you in danger?"

"No. I don't think so. I don't know."

"Because if you are, get the fuck out of here. Go someplace no one can find you until it all blows over."

"I can't do that. I've got the run to finish."

"Screw the damn run. It's just a show. Your understudy can go on. He'll be glad of the experience. You're replaceable in a musical. You're not replaceable in life. Elijah doesn't want your understudy. It's you he loves. Look after number one. Always."

"There are only two more days," Daniel said firmly. "I won't run away."

"Then for God's sake, take care. You're not a cat with nine lives. You survived with a few injuries before. You might not be so lucky this time."

* * * *

Following the show on Friday, Max arranged a late-night dinner for Daniel, Elijah and Ben at a small Greek restaurant on Talbot Road.

"Just the four of us," she said. "We've got the big party Saturday, but I want to do something small, just for us."

The restaurant was a favorite of Max's. It had opened in Blackpool over twenty years ago, and she'd made a habit of eating there whenever she was in town. She'd already taken Daniel for dinner four times during the run. The food was always superb. He couldn't wait for Elijah to try it.

"Remember, I am half Greek," Elijah said, when he told him of Max's plan. "I grew up on that food. It'll have to be something special to impress me."

"You'll be blown away," Daniel assured him. "Even if you are *Celebrity Top Cook* these days."

"Shush. That's a secret."

The owners had agreed to stay open late to accommodate the booking and it was almost midnight when they arrived. Getting out of the theater had become a major trial. The queues at the stage door were bigger than ever, compounded by the police officers assigned to watch Daniel and the ever-present photographers and reporters.

"I called ahead," Max told them in the car. "Requested they put us on a table away from the window, well out of sight."

Glancing through the back window of the car, Daniel saw his police escort close behind, followed by a couple of paparazzi on motorbikes. On arrival, the owners ushered them inside, together with the police officers, before locking the front door. The cops took a table near the front, affording the group a little privacy.

The table was prepared with two bottles of Greek red wine, open and ready.

"Do the honours," Max said to Ben, indicating that he should pour the drinks.

Elijah sipped the wine and smacked his lips appreciatively. "Very nice."

"Don't sound so surprised." Max chuckled. "This is my favorite place in the whole world."

The owners had gone to town, setting the mood for Max's supper party, dimming the lights and putting out candles. A selection of bread and cold meats were brought to the table. Daniel helped himself to a slice of olive bread. Fresh, still warm from the oven, it tasted delicious.

Across the table, Max and Ben cozied up together. The speed at which their relationship had developed surprised him, though he knew it shouldn't. He knew better than anyone the reality of love at first sight. Max and Ben had known each other four days now. Daniel had fallen for Elijah after one. They'd slept together on the second day, consummating the deep feelings they had for each other. And on the third, Oliver Gill had tried to kill him. And Elijah sat beside him now, proof that love could thrive in the hardest circumstances.

He was happy for them. If something good could come out of this awful week, let it be their relationship.

"A toast," Max said, raising her glass. "To the end of a successful run and to new beginnings."

"New beginnings," they said, clinking glasses.

"The producers have been on at me again about signing on for London," Daniel said.

"They have?" Elijah said. "Don't they think you've got enough to worry about right now? You don't need this pressure."

"It's okay," Daniel assured him. "I understand. They're under pressure themselves. They've got obligations to fulfill."

"Obligations my arse," Elijah muttered. "They're taking advantage."

"They offered to double what they're paying me now."

"Good. What did you tell them?" Max asked.

"I said maybe. I'm not ready to make the commitment. I told them to ask me again in a few weeks. I'm not playing hard for extra money. The fee isn't important. I'd understand if they want to find another actor. They know that. If they find someone who wants to do it, they should book him. I won't be offended."

"I will," Max said. "You're my leading man. I don't want anyone else."

"He needs a break," Elijah insisted.

"I do," Daniel admitted. "Maybe after Christian's funeral, or when the cops make an arrest, I'll be in a better place to think about the future. Right now, I just want to get through tomorrow, do the last two shows, make them great, then nothing. I'll probably sleep through all of next week."

"I thought you were going to take a holiday," Ben said.

"We are," Elijah said, dipping a chunk of bread in olive oil.

"But he won't tell me where we're going," Daniel said, nudging him playfully.

"It's a surprise. Besides, the less people who know about it, the less likely they are to find us."

"Good thinking," Ben said.

"What about you?" Elijah asked him. "Daniel's not the only one at risk here. You could be in danger too. What are your plans?"

"Business as usual," Ben said with a shrug. "I took this week off but have to get back to work on Monday. I'm writing with a producer friend in Manchester. So, I'm sticking to that plan."

Max put her hand on top of his. "I wish you wouldn't. Let's take off like these guys. I have nothing else to do after tomorrow. We can get out of the way. At least for a few days until the cops get a handle on the case."

Ben shook his head. "What if they don't? I can't hide away forever. Life has to get back to normal. Besides, I don't think running away will solve anything. Whoever is behind all this—and I do believe someone is, it's not just paranoia on our part—well, that psycho is prepared to play a long game. There's about six weeks between Luke's death and Christian's murder. If they were looking to whack us quickly, they'd have done it by now. They could have gotten us anytime, when we least expected it. I think they want us to be frightened. Always looking over our shoulder. That's part of their game, to make us anxious and jumpy. Well, I've decided I won't play."

Listening to Ben, Daniel realized he was right. The killer had had every opportunity to get to him. He could have struck anytime this summer. Running away wouldn't fix it.

He'd spent six months in hiding after Oliver's death. Well, no more. Like Ben, he intended to get on with his life.

"Okay, I'm going to speak to the producers in the morning," he said. "Before the matinee. I've decided. I am doing the London run. Max, you've got your leading man."

* * * *

Close to one in the morning, Sonny Rock stood on the promenade, looking out to sea. He heard the water hitting the beach yards beneath him, but everything beyond the edge of the railing was black. The darkness drew him and there was nowhere darker than the sea at night.

He wore one of his regular disguises, a peaked cap pulled low over his brow on top of a greasy wig. Combined with the goofy false teeth that changed the lines of his face, his own mother would fail to recognize him. In dirty jeans and scruffy bomber jacket, no one ever gave him a second glance.

At two minutes to one, he inserted a new SIM into his cheap mobile and turned on the device. The call came right on the hour.

"Everything set?" the caller asked.

"This time tomorrow it'll be over," Sonny said.

There was a long pause before, "Make it hurt. Maximum damage, maximin pain. I want them to suffer."

Sonny chuckled. "You get that as standard. No extra charge."

Chapter Fifteen

Elijah lay awake, listening to the sound of the sea. Dull light penetrated the heavy curtains of the hotel bedroom. He could have gotten up. There was zero chance of getting back to sleep, but the bed was warm and comfortable and almost as nice as the naked body next to him.

Daniel slept on his side, facing the other away. The curve of his spine and the fullness of his buttocks pressed against Elijah's side. He breathed easily, still asleep. *Let him rest*, Elijah thought, *he needs it with two shows today*. Elijah wished he could join him in peaceful sleep. A lie-in with the man he loved was exactly what he needed, but it wasn't to be today.

He'd endured a restless night with long periods of wakefulness. When he'd finally drifted off, his sleep had been plagued by nightmares, vivid dreams he found difficult to rouse from or shake off. The images and negative emotions lingered long after he opened his eyes. He'd lain awake since five, unable to ditch the feeling that something was wrong.

Things were very wrong. That was clear already. *Two men murdered — how much worse can it get?* What he felt this morning was different, more like a premonition, a sense of dread for something that had yet to happen. And throughout the night, his thoughts returned to one thing — Oliver Gill.

In the rational light of morning, he thought these current events couldn't be connected to Oliver's death. But in the depths of the dark, he couldn't see how they weren't. The reason eluded him, but he knew, with every fiber of himself, that there had to be one.

Just get through today. That's what matters.

Elijah had booked a cottage for next week. Up north, in County Durham, far from anywhere. First thing tomorrow, he would take Daniel there. High in the hills, miles from the nearest town, no one would find them. Its remoteness would keep them safe. The fewer people aware of his plan the better. He wouldn't say anything to Daniel until they were on the way. There'd be no chance of him letting slip to someone in the crew about where they were going. Complete secrecy — it was the only way to be sure of Daniel's safety.

Elijah had booked the cottage in his brother's name and arranged with the owner to pay in cash upon arrival. He'd left nothing to chance. Until the police knew what they doing, who they were searching for, Daniel had to disappear.

In the long hours before dawn, Elijah tried to think of every eventuality. He'd almost lost Daniel once before. There was no way he'd let it happen again.

Eventually, he rolled onto his side, cuddling in behind Daniel. He slid his arm around Daniel's waist and his hand inadvertently brushed the tip of his morning erection. Elijah snuggled closer, pressing his chest into Daniel's back, resting his chin on his shoulder. He carefully curled his hand around Daniel's hard dick, luxuriating in its length and thickness.

You're the luckiest man alive, he thought, pressing his hips against the warm, naked mounds of Daniel's arse. The worries of the night were soon forgotten as his cock grew stiff, nudging Daniel's crack, parting his flesh. The crevice was hot and sweaty.

"That's a nice way to wake me up," Daniel drawled.

"Sorry," Elijah said. "I didn't mean to disturb you, but my cock had other ideas."

Daniel chuckled, straightening his legs and leaning into Elijah's body. He clenched his buttocks, squeezing Elijah's dick between them. "What time is it?"

"Almost eight, I think." Elijah kissed the back of his neck. "How did you sleep?"

"Good," he answered. His cock twitched. Elijah drew his hand along its full length and teased the moist head with the tips of his fingers. Daniel gasped. "Keep doing that."

"This?" Elijah teased, stroking the tiny triangle of skin right beneath the opening of Daniel's dick. So soft and sticky. So very sensitive. Pre-cum oozed onto his fingertips.

His own cock seeped just as fluidly. He ground his hips and it slid smoothly up and down Daniel's cleft in a lube of sweat and pre-cum.

The concerns of last night became irrelevant. Nothing mattered but the man beside him.

"I want to fuck you," Elijah murmured, holding him even tighter.

Daniel reached behind, grabbing Elijah's dick. He squeezed milky pre-cum to the tip, rubbing it all over the smooth head. Elijah shuddered. They rarely made love without lubricant, but sometimes, when they were both so horny, like now, it wasn't necessary. Their bodies required nothing extra.

Daniel guided Elijah's cock to his arse, maneuvering the head to his opening. Elijah pushed, testing the resistance. If there was any opposition he would stop and lube the way properly. Daniel opened without a hitch, issuing a moan that was pure pleasure.

Encourage, Elijah wrapped an arm around his chest and pushed in all the way. He put his lips on Daniel's neck, inhaling the sleepy smell of his hair, and rooted himself inside the fiery core. His man. His responsibility. He would love him and take care of him.

In that moment, they had never been closer.

Elijah made love to him with long, fluid motions, pleasuring Daniel with every inch of his cock. He licked the sweat that coated the nape of his neck. Still lying on his side, Daniel raised his legs, hooking his elbows behind his knees so Elijah could go deeper into him.

"Oh, yes." Daniel sighed as the head of Elijah's cock poked his prostate.

Elijah held him tighter, knowing he'd reached that special place. He thrust, stroking the nub of pleasure with each inward stroke. Daniel reached around, grabbed the back of Elijah's head and pulled him closer so they could kiss.

Daniel was close to the point of no return. Elijah recognized the helpless pitch in his voice, signaling the end. He moved his hand back to Daniel's cock, wrapping his fist around it, squeezing and tugging. Daniel inhaled ragged breaths, coming closer and closer until hot semen erupted from his cock and dribbled down Elijah's hand. The contractions caused his arse to tighten, tipping Elijah over the edge. With Daniel's semen coating his fingers, he deposited his own inside him.

"Oh, fuck," Daniel gasped when they were done. "Wake me up like that every morning."

"No objection here," Elijah said, rolling his hips to stir up Daniel's butt.

"Oh, God, stop," he pleaded. "I've got to dance today. I won't be able to walk if you keep that up."

Elijah laughed and hugged him tight, remaining inside. "I love you."

"I love you too," Daniel said, pushing back his hips.

They lay there for a while, reluctant to break the connection.

"Do you still feel the same as you did last night?" he asked at last.

"About doing the show? Yes. I'm taking it to London. Probably not for long. I'll see what Rachel and Alisha have to say about it today. If they'll agree to a short contract, say three or four months, then I'll do it. I don't want to be tied in for longer than that. You're not mad, are you?"

"Of course not. Why would I be?"

"Because I decided without telling you first."

"Hey," Elijah said softly. "I'm your boyfriend, not your keeper. You don't need my permission for anything. I'll support you whatever you decide."

"I just want a normal life," Daniel said. "For me, that means work. I've got to do something. If I have too much time on my hands, I'll go mad. I know I will. I've come pretty close to it already this year. No more. You were the one who said we should go back to work, and you were right."

"That was before what happened to Christian and Luke. I just want you to be safe. I couldn't cope if anything happened to you."

Daniel rolled over in bed, wrapping his arms around Elijah's neck. Even now, first thing in the morning, he looked extraordinarily handsome.

"Nothing will happen. We've got each other. That's everything."

* * * *

Elijah accompanied Daniel to the theater for the afternoon show. He knew Daniel would be busy for most of the time but couldn't shake the uneasy feeling that had kept him awake. He intended to keep Daniel close today. Very close.

A crowd had already assembled at the stage door when they arrived. Flowers and cards were thrust at Daniel as soon as he stepped out of the car. Elijah put a protective arm around his shoulder and tried to shield him from the eager well-wishers.

"Take it easy," Daniel said, as Elijah attempted to cover him. "They just want to say hello."

Undeterred, Elijah marched him toward the stage door, where a uniformed cop and a couple of theater guys kept the entrance clear. He didn't doubt that among the hordes of people, there were plenty of fans and supporters, but Daniel's name had been in the news all week and that had also drawn the morbidly curious and the gawkers to the scene. *Who knows who else is out there?*

It was no time to take chances or get complacent.

While Daniel went to see the producers about the London transfer, Elijah helped himself to a bottle of water from the minibar in his dressing room and flopped onto the sofa, checking his phone. Though the cops were all over it, he'd been keeping a close eye on Daniel's social media accounts, checking the comments and messages, weeding out the trolls. It was unlikely Christian's killer would announce himself via a bitchy tweet, but Elijah read them just the same. With Oliver Gill, he'd been blind to the threat in front of them. He'd make damn sure that never happened again.

Today it was all good. There were lots of comments from fans wishing him well for the final two shows. Nothing hostile or aggressive.

He looked up as Joe, the young costume assistant, entered the room.

"Oh, sorry," the boy flustered. "I...I saw Daniel with Rachel and Alisha. I didn't know you were in here, I would have knocked first."

"Just as well I'm decent," Elijah teased.

Joe's eyes widened and he looked at Elijah uncertainly. "I've, er, walked in on worse things."

Elijah laughed. "I bet you have. Backstage on a big show, you must have seen it all."

"I'd never tell," the boy said, regaining his composure. He removed the protective cellophane from Daniel's costume.

Joe wore cargo shorts and a baggy T-shirt. It seemed to be his customary wardrobe. Elijah couldn't remember seeing him in anything else. He was an odd little guy. Slender with a huge blond coif. Attractive, but not Elijah's type. He liked a manly man, like Daniel. Joe was too twinky, too boyish.

But there was no malice in the lad. Lying awake, in the middle of the night, he'd wondered about him, became suspicious of him. Anyone with access to Daniel was a suspect. But Joe was a nice kid. Probably a bit naïve and inexperienced—he seemed to know nothing of life outside his home town—but he appeared harmless.

"Are you looking forward to the party tonight?" Joe asked with wide, excitable eyes.

"To be honest, I'd forgotten about it. With everything else that's going on, I can't say I'm in much of a party mood."

Joe's smile wavered. "You are going, aren't you? You and Daniel, I mean. You must go. It's the wrap. Everyone will be there. We might not see you again after tonight."

Elijah remembered what Daniel had told him the other night, that Joe had a crush on him. Maybe he was right. The boy looked at him with hopeful eyes.

"Wouldn't miss it for anything," he said.

Joe smiled brightly again. "Good. We're gonna have a fantastic time. One thing you can say about Blackpool folk, we know how to party."

"I don't doubt it," Elijah said, sitting up straight, looking at Joe with a keener eye. He wasn't a bad-looking lad. Probably a late bloomer. In another year or two, he'd grow into his looks and take his pick of any man he fancied. Right now, his confidence was fragile. Elijah had been the same at that age. "Do you live round there?" he asked.

"Not far, just out of town. On a good day I can walk it, but I usually get the bus."

"You're not walking home tonight, are you?" Elijah left the rest of the thought unspoken — *After what happened to Christian.*

"Depends how lucky I get," Joe said, looking at him meaningfully for a second, before busying himself with Daniel's stage shoes. "I might stay over or get a taxi."

"Be careful," Elijah said. "Whatever you do, don't take unnecessary chances."

* * * *

During the first act of the matinee, Elijah met Ben in the theater bar. They had originally planned to watch the show, but it was sold out. There wasn't a spare seat for either of today's performances. They could have watched from the wings, but Elijah knew they would only get in the way.

"I'm starving," Ben said, grabbing a food menu as soon as they found a table. "Max tells me the gourmet burgers in here are to die for."

"Max doesn't strike me as a burger girl," Elijah said, sipping his beer.

"She says 'everything in moderation' these days. I'm proud of her, not being afraid of food anymore. She had serious problems in the past."

Elijah nodded. Max LaFranchi's eating disorders were well-documented. He remembered the lurid headlines in the *News of the World* when he was a kid, when the slime-ball tabloid reveled in her misfortune and ill health. At least Max had the last laugh. She was a survivor, still around, while the gutter-press rag had been consigned to history. "Did you know who Max was before you met her?"

"I remembered seeing her on the telly when I was a kid, and all that, but I never followed her career. Not until Christian suggested we come and see the show. Then I had a little look at some of her stuff online. But I never expected to have such a connection when I met her. She blew me away."

When he spoke about Max, Ben's face lit up. Elijah knew exactly how he felt. From the moment he'd met Daniel, his own emotions had been just as strong. "So, what's next for the two of you? If you're going back to work on Monday, how do you plan to stay in touch?"

Ben sipped his beer and licked the foam from his top lip. "We'll get together next weekend. Take it from there."

"Can you wait that long?"

The smile wavered. "Got no choice. Until we know who's responsible for killing Christian and Luke, and what they want, I can't take any chances. The more time I spend with Max, the more danger she'll be in. She wants to come to Manchester on Monday, but I won't let her take that risk. It's safer if she stays away."

"Max is a determined woman, used to getting what she wants. She might not stay away."

"It's not an option. I want her with me. You've no idea how much. But the risks are too high." He nodded at the pair of police officers stationed by the door. "They won't be there forever. In a day or two, if nothing else happens, they will downgrade the threat and stop looking out for us. I can take care of myself but can't guarantee Max's safety when she's with me."

"Maybe she wants to take care of you. Max is a wealthy woman. She can afford private security."

"She's already suggested that, but I'm not taking hand-outs. This bastard has a beef with me, not Max. She doesn't have to be involved."

"But she wants to be involved with you," Elijah said. "If she's prepared to take the risk."

Ben shook his head. "As long as there's a risk, she has to keep a distance."

* * * *

At the next table, so close he could hear every word, Sonny Rock pretended to be busy with his mobile. He was wearing a new disguise, far different from the slovenly character he'd presented this week, washed and clean-shaven, with a pair of smart glasses, a navy cashmere pullover, Hugo Boss jeans and Ted Baker shoes. He held himself confidently, shoulders back, jaw thrust forward, the image of an entitled, modern man. No one would recognize him.

He listened intently to the conversation next to him.

Pathetic. These losers don't know the meaning of risk. They don't understand how close to death they are.

Listening to them gave Sonny another hard-on.

They had no idea of the real danger they were in. Talking about their plans and precautions. Whatever they did was a waste of time. It was *his* call. He'd decide when and where. He could take either one of them at any time and they couldn't stop him.

Sonny was a man of action, of violence. They were merely reactionaries. He would always have the edge on them.

"After talking to her last night, Max understands," the black man said. "She'll wait for me until it's over."

Sonny's face stayed granite hard, but inside he laughed. He had no interest in the woman. *All this crap about keeping her safe.* She didn't matter. Max LaFranchi played no part in the plan. He wanted Daniel and Ben.

And Elijah.

There was another member of Overload living in America. He could wait. A small coda to his run of murders. Sonny would get to him eventually. Right now, he had two of his intended targets in sight. So close he could smell their aftershave.

In what order should I kill them? It hardly mattered — they were all marked for death — but he could have a little fun in the process. Like a cat tormenting a nest of mice, Sonny strove for maximum impact, maximum terror.

Daniel was the prize. The end game. Sonny's instructions were clear. Daniel must not only die, he had to suffer.

Killing this pair first, his friend and his lover, would guarantee Daniel's grief before his own end came.

Ben got up and went over to the bar with a food menu. Sonny kept his face turned to his phone while he studied Elijah with sideways eyes. He was a big guy. Strongly built. They all were, but their size didn't concern Sonny. A midget could bring down a giant when they knew exactly how. Elijah sipped his beer and glanced around the bar, probably wondering whether any of these people here had it in for him. *Let him wonder.* No one paid him any obvious attention.

Sonny remembered watching him a few years ago on a BBC sketch show called *Shades of England.* Comedy held no appeal for Sonny, but this was different. Off the wall — witty and stupid in equal measures. He'd caught a late-night repeat while staying in a hotel. After one episode, he'd been hooked and set the whole series to record. Elijah had been one of three actors in an ensemble. He was the funniest of the group. Watching him on the show, Sonny had never imaged he'd be stalking him, planning his death. He used to like Elijah a lot.

Funny how things turn out.

Now Sonny had a job to do.

Ben came back from the bar with two fresh pints. "The food will take about twenty minutes, they say."

"I'm gonna go to the loo," Elijah said, sliding off his seat.

Sonny watched him go. The bar was quiet. Most people were in the theater with a straggle of tourists hanging round the concourse of the Winter Gardens. Elijah drew a few admiring glances as he went, but no one bothered him. Sonny waited a couple of beats, making sure nobody had followed, before slipping his phone into his pocket and getting up. He took his empty glass with him.

Ben, absorbed in his own mobile, paid no attention.

The cops were stationed at the main entrance. Sonny knew he could walk right past them without drawing attention. This time tomorrow he'd look quite different again, but why take the risk when he didn't need to? He exited the bar through the right doorway, dumping his glass on a busy table before cutting through the empty Spanish Hall to enter the main concourse beside the theater.

The show had yet to break. A bored-looking girl attended the ice cream kiosk, while an older woman replenished the merchandise stall ahead of the interval. Neither looked up as he passed.

Sonny descended a wide flight of stairs to the men's toilet in the basement.

This was unplanned. One of those spontaneous opportunities he'd learned to recognize, knowing when to take advantage of them. He'd followed Elijah and Ben to the bar with little thought for what he'd do to them. But when Elijah had left alone for the bathroom, he'd taken his chance.

Sonny knew every inch of the Winter Gardens. He'd spent weeks casing the building. When he'd learned Daniel would be working here all summer, he'd known this was the place. The men's basement toilets were large with plenty of cubicles and urinals. Once they had been a popular haunt for gays and wayward husbands cruising for cock, but dating apps had damped that pursuit. No one had to risk a punch in the face or arrest for a casual bit of fun. The huge underground toilets were empty most of the time.

Making them the perfect location for a kill.

As he reached the bottom of the steps and entered, Sonny's cock remained hard. The expectation of violence was better than foreplay. Carnage and savagery beat sex hands-down when it came to getting off. His senses were on fire.

The urinals were empty. Elijah must have gone into a cubicle.

There was no one else around.

Perfect.

This is it. A golden opportunity.

He would have to be quick. He'd intended a prolonged death for Elijah Mann, but like Christian, circumstances demanded rapid action. He might only have a few seconds.

That was all it would take.

A sharp blow to the throat, crushing the windpipe. He'd shove Elijah into one of the stalls and watch him asphyxiate. It would take a few minutes for him to die, but it would be quiet. Sonny could enjoy those moments as he struggled for life. Watch that handsome face blotch and bulge. A small pleasure compared to what Sonny has planned, but better than nothing.

He stood still and listened.

A sudden stream of piss hit the bowl in a cubicle to his right. Rising to the balls of his feet, Sonny followed the sound, three doors down. He stopped, silent, outside the door, and listened. There was no sound other than the splash of Elijah emptying his bladder. They were alone. He was sure of it.

Sonny's cock throbbed with anticipation. His underpants were damp with pre-cum. He might relieve himself inside them as he watched Elijah die. There'd be no DNA evidence if he contained the load. The idea turned him on even more.

Inside the cubicle, Elijah stopped pissing.

Listening, Sonny focused, tuning out the ambient noise, concentrating fully on Elijah.

He heard the rustle of clothing. The flush of the toilet. Elijah turning in the cubicle.

The lock was drawn back.

The door opened.

This is it. Concentrate. Only one shot. Sharp and fast.

Elijah stepped forward, unprepared to find someone standing there.

He looked at Sonny, startled.

Sonny hesitated a moment, enjoying the confused look on his face.

Anticipation is almost as good as the kill.

His dick leaked thick and fast.

"Oh," Elijah said, "excuse me."

He'd lifted his head, offering his neck. Sonny's eyes fixed on the target. He stiffened his hand, ready to strike.

One blow was all it would take.

Take your last breath, my friend. You're about to go down for good.

Chapter Sixteen

Elijah jolted unexpectedly as he opened the door on the stranger. The last thing he'd expected was to find someone standing there. The bathroom was empty and there must have been twenty other cubicles this guy could use. The man stared straight at him.

Do I know him? Elijah wondered, staring back.

The man was maybe forty. He had one of those faces that made it hard to guess his age. Narrow eyes, with glasses sitting on a thin nose. Good-looking in a kind of battered way.

As he looked into the man's eyes, a cold sensation gripped his spine. His heart raced and adrenaline surged, like the impulses of a cornered beast. He looked at the man, at the dead expression on his face, and knew with full certainty that he was responsible for killing Luke and Christian.

He didn't know how — it was instinct, but here was the one they'd been looking for.

The cruel suggestion of a smile flicked the corners of the man's mouth, like a cat about to toy with a mouse.

He knows that I know. And in the next moment, an overwhelming realization. *I'm going to die. Right now, here in this toilet. I won't see Daniel again. It's over.*

It was a second, two seconds, strung out beyond endurance. All his senses intensified. He heard the drip of the cistern and the rumble of the water pipes. The acrid stink of piss and damp seared his nostrils.

He registered minute details about the man's face. Broken thread veins around his nose, a random gray hair in his eyebrow, the shaving rash on his throat. More dreadful than anything — the knowledge he had frozen. Elijah wanted to move, to lash out, to smash the bastard's nose into his face, but his body betrayed him.

Another second stretched to infinity. The man snorted and his eyes narrowed further. His shoulders pulled back, the tension building through his arm. Elijah had never known a moment draw out so far.

This is how it feels to stare death in the face. And for death to stare right back.

I'm not ready for the end.

Suddenly they were not alone. There were footsteps on the stairs, laughter and voices coming closer.

Time snapped back into focus.

The matinee had broken for the interval, and the spell that had paralyzed Elijah lost its grip. He raised his arm to block the stranger's assault, but nothing came. The man turned and ran across the bathroom floor. As the theater crowd parted, he lost himself in their throng.

Elijah gripped the stall door, aware of how close he'd come to losing everything. The man was after him. Wanted to kill him. No doubt about it.

Who the hell is he?

He took a couple of deep breaths, getting his head together.

"Are you okay, mate?" A middle-aged man, on his way to the next cubicle, looked at him with concern. "You don't look well."

Elijah nodded. "I'm fine," he forced out.

The man moved on, looking back at him, unconvinced.

All at once Elijah rushed into action. *Ben*. He was still upstairs, blind to the danger he was in. He raced across the bathroom, almost slipping on the wet floor, and collided with a young dad leading his son to a stall.

"Watch it," the man yelled angrily.

Elijah didn't stop to apologize. He reached the bottom of the stairs. There was no sign of the stranger in the crowd that moved toward him. Battling against the tide of people, he shoved upward. The bastard was getting away. If he hadn't frozen, behaved like a such a victim, he could have stopped him.

The lobby and concourse were packed as he reached the top. People stood around and talked. They ate ice cream and looked at their theater programs. They praised the show, oblivious to the drama playing out in front of them. Elijah pushed through, ignoring the furious looks and incensed comments directed at him.

The cops were still stationed at the entrance to the bar. He gestured furiously for them to follow him, hurrying inside, searching for Ben.

Ben sat right where he'd left him, sipping his beer.

"Oh, thank God." Elijah sighed, finally coming to a stop.

"What's wrong?" Ben said, getting to his feet and taking Elijah's arm.

The police officers were right beside him.

"He's here," Elijah said, out of breath. "In the toilet. Bastard must have followed me in."

"Who?" Ben gripped him tighter.

"The killer."

"Are you sure?" The larger of the cops asked. "Where you attacked?"

"If the show hadn't broken for the interval, I'd be dead." He described the man to the cops and told them what he was wearing. The second officer put it out on the radio before he'd finished.

"Stay here, the pair of you. Don't leave the bar till we get back." The cops raced into the foyer.

Ben put an arm on his shoulder. "You're shaking. C'mon, sit. What the hell happened? Who was it?"

Elijah fell into the chair. He grabbed his beer and gulped rapidly. His thirst was near unquenchable. He saw the way the glass trembled and took it in two hands. "I don't know who he was but I'm pretty sure it was the guy who sat there earlier." He pointed at the next table. "I didn't pay much attention at the time, but I'm certain that's who it was."

"What happened?"

He gave Ben the details. "He was right there when I opened the door, in my face. I knew the second I saw him that he'd come for me. He was completely cold. Like looking into an abyss of hatred. But I saw the intent in his eyes. I'm sure he wanted to do me right there but then all these people came in."

They sat in silence for a minute, digesting what had happened. Around them, the bar filled up. There were plenty of happy people, enjoying the afternoon show.

"It makes no sense," Ben said at last. "What made him come after you? You weren't in the band. You had nothing to do with Overload until you met Daniel."

"That's what I'm afraid of," Elijah said. As he ran it through his mind, rearranging the jigsaw pieces, it began to make sense. Twisted and fucked up, but sense all the same. "This guy doesn't hold a grudge against Overload. It's Daniel that he wants. Christian and Luke, I think they were just a twisted message. He wants to hurt Daniel by hurting those close to him first."

"So who the fuck is he?" Ben cried.

"I have no idea. That's the scary part."

* * * *

Daniel took Max's hand for the final curtain call of the afternoon show. The noise coming up from the auditorium was deafening. The audience didn't want them to leave the stage and weren't afraid to show it. The entire crowd stood and cheered.

In the orchestra pit Andre, the conductor, dropped his pants and mooned the stage, parting the cheeks of his huge arse to give them an eyeful of his hairy crack. Max howled her appreciation as the curtain fell. Practical tricks were par for the course on the last day of any show.

"God knows what they've got planned tonight." Daniel laughed.

"You need to take your butt to the barber," Max yelled into the pit. "Show me again when've done the crack and sac."

"Loan me your lady shave and I'll take care of it," Andre hollered back.

"Don't encourage him," Daniel said, leading her to the wings. "You do realize we'll have to look at his shaven-haven later?"

"Oh, I hope so. And plenty more besides."

They walked the backstage run together. Daniel's nerves prickled. The show had been off the scale this afternoon. He'd given it everything, immersing himself in his character for a few hours to ignore the challenges of real life. It had worked too. He'd realized partway through the first act that he'd made the right decision committing to the London production. He genuinely loved this show. Loved his role. Loved working with the cast and crew, especially Max. Apart from Elijah, work was everything to him. No one would take it away.

"I'm soooo looking forward to the party later," Max drawled, undoing the top button of her costume. "A lot of drinks, some dancing, a chance to let my hair down."

"Let your hair down?" Daniel laughed, nudging her elbow. "When *don't* you let it down? You got out every weekend."

"That's not that same. A party is different. And a wrap party is the best of all. I can see I need to educate you in the finer arts of the wrap. Some of the wildest nights of my life have been at the end of a run."

Daniel didn't doubt it, and despite everything, he shared her excitement. The party was just what he needed. It had been a traumatic week and his immediate future seemed more precarious than ever, but tonight he planned to enjoy himself. When he faced reality again on Sunday morning, he intended to do it through the blur of a hangover. "Let's get a bottle of vodka on ice ready for our arrival. Screw champagne. I need to get shitfaced tonight."

"Now you're talking. And make that two bottles. The first will only be enough to get us started."

As they turned the corner to their dressing room, he saw straight away that something was wrong. The cops, previously stationed at the stage door, were now right outside his room, while another officer stood guard at Max's door. *Shit. What now?*

He darted for the door.

Elijah. Oh, God, something's happened to him.

As he burst inside, the relief was instant. Elijah and Ben were sitting on the sofa, glum-faced but both unhurt. They smiled as he approached but their eyes were full of trouble.

"What happened?" Daniel asked.

"Nothing," they answered together.

"You're a couple of lousy liars," he replied. They both looked completely wired and the anxiety in the room was tangible.

"What's with all the cops?" Max asked, coming up behind him. "There's one outside my room now. Why do I need protection?"

Elijah shrugged. The action was anything but natural. "It's nothing. Trust us."

"Well, you're acting like it's something," Max snapped. "Do I have to drag it out of you?"

"Darling, please." Ben stepped forward and put both hands on her shoulders, gently squeezing. "Trust us."

Daniel looked from Ben to Elijah. Neither of them would meet his eyes for more than a second. "What the hell? You can't do this. What has happened? Do the cops have fresh information?"

Elijah's shoulders drooped. "Kind of." He took Daniel's hands in his, moving real close. "Do you trust me?"

"Yes. But—"

"No buts. Do you?" he pressed.

"Yes."

"Then trust me now. Ben and I, we'll tell you everything, both of you, tonight. You've got one more show to get through. That's what you need to focus on. The people who've bought tickets, your fans, they deserve your best. *You* deserve to give your best. Enjoy it. It's your show. Your night. We're not going anywhere. We'll be here the whole time. And when you're done, we'll explain everything."

"Whatever it is, it must be pretty bad if you can't say now," Max retorted.

"It's nothing that will change between now and ten o'clock," Ben told her softly, caressing her chin. "Believe us. Do the last performance and everything will be all right."

Max's eyes shot to Daniel. "I don't like this. No, scratch that. I fucking hate this."

He didn't see how they had a choice. They had a show to do and, whatever the hell was going on, these two had already planned how to handle it. And Elijah was the one person, maybe the only person, he trusted. "All right," Daniel said at last. "But answer me one thing first. Are you hurt?"

Elijah kissed his brow. "Not at all. I promise you. I'm fine."

"Okay." He sighed wearily. "I'll do it on one condition. The minute we leave the stage, we're coming right back here and you're going to tell us everything. Before the party, before we take our bloody makeup off, you tell us what's going on."

"Deal," Elijah said.

"Deal," Ben echoed.

Daniel hugged Elijah tight and, burrowing his face in his neck, he inhaled his warm, familiar smell. This was worse than that night on the *Anthem*. When Oliver attacked him, he'd known nothing until the moment it went down. Now someone else was after them and he knew they were coming. They were already here. And this time it wasn't just him at risk. Elijah, Ben, maybe even Max, they were all in danger.

Someone intended to hurt them, and he had no idea who.

But there was one thought he couldn't shake. Whoever was hunting them, they were connected to Oliver. It made no sense, there was no evidence to link them, but Daniel knew in his heart the connection was there. He hoped they found it before it was too late.

* * * *

Sonny Rock sat in his room at The Majestic Hotel and looked fixedly at the sea. He'd checked into the hotel on Thursday, using another fake ID, but had slept in the old flat until today. Outside, the sky was a deepening shade of blue and white caps crowned the slate-gray waves. Sonny saw none of it, his focus directed inward.

He'd been sloppy. Thinking he could deal with Elijah in the bathroom, without planning, without thinking ahead. He should have known the matinee was due to break. The bathroom didn't offer the privacy and cover he needed to do the job right. He'd acted like an amateur.

Now Elijah had seen him. Could recognize his face.

Worse than that, he knew Sonny was close. He'd be on guard more than ever. They all would. The factor of surprise had gone. Lost. Elijah wouldn't let Daniel out of his sight now. They'd have cops close to the them at all times.

But Sonny had made a vow he wouldn't break. A commitment.

They would all die tonight.

He'd make sure of that.

Chapter Seventeen

Elijah explained everything using simple, concise language. It needed no exaggeration. For Daniel, it was scary enough.

They were in his dressing room again. Max and Daniel were still in costume, hot from their last performance, and listened without interruption, while he spoke. Ben leaned against the dresser, for the moment saying nothing. An uneasy sensation tightened in Daniel's belly. He clutched his hands together to stop them from shaking. The killer had come for Elijah that very afternoon, while he'd strutted about the stage, oblivious.

They were living a nightmare, which was getting worse every moment.

When Elijah finished, they sat in silence. Daniel struggled to digest all he'd heard. His chest constricted, a sensation that his heart and lungs were being crushed, and he recognized the initial stages of a panic attack. He wouldn't give in to it. This was no time to lose his shit.

"Pour me a drink, would you?" he asked Ben. "Scotch. No ice. Don't skimp on the measure."

Max cleared her throat. "I'll have the same," she said.

Ben pulled a bottle from the bar and poured the liquor splashily into two crystal tumblers. "Here."

Daniel's hand shook as he brought the glass to his lips. He ignored the tremors and drank deep, letting the burning liquid flood his gullet, waiting for it to take effect. Elijah's story confirmed what he already suspected. He and Ben were not the only targets of the killer. He'd come for all of them. Max might be okay. He suspected the link between all of this was Oliver, either through Overload or the *Atlantic Anthem*. Max had no connection to either of them, apart from her relationship with Ben. But this guy was obviously a psychopath — just like Oliver. They couldn't rule anything out.

The mood was broken by an unexpected knock on the door. Joe entered without waiting for an answer.

"Oh, sorry," he said, taken back. "Do you want me to come back later?"

Joe had changed his clothes during the final act of the show and was all ready for the party in jeans and a tight-fitting T-shirt. The scent of his cologne threatened to overpower the flavor of their scotch.

Daniel shook his head. "It's fine, Joe. I'll take care of myself tonight. Get yourself to the party. Have fun."

Joe hesitated. "I don't mind waiting. I'll get in trouble if the clothes aren't put away properly."

"It's okay. I won't run away with them. Really."

"You, er, you are coming to the party, aren't you?"

Daniel forced a smile. "Wouldn't miss it. We'll see you there in a little while."

"And I expect a dance," Max said, with false enthusiasm.

Joe looked uncertainly from Daniel to Elijah, before nodding and backing out of the room. "Okay, I'll let everyone know you're on the way."

The whiskey eased the tight knot in Daniel's chest. "The last thing I feel like is partying." He raised his glass for a refill.

"We have to go," Max said. "To show our faces at least."

"What did the police say about this man today?" Daniel asked Elijah.

"I spoke to DI Ritson tonight. The guy didn't leave a glass behind in the bar. He knew what he was doing. They dusted the table for prints, but it's riddled with them. The chances of getting a match are minuscule. They've put out a description to all cops, but again, slim chance of anyone spotting him."

"Don't they have any idea who he is?" Max asked.

"None."

"In my opinion, this all ties back to Oliver," Daniel said. "The *Anthem* and the band, they're what link us to him. This man must also be connected in some way, don't you think?"

"You mean, his dad, or someone?" Max asked.

Ben shook his head. "There was no dad. No mother either that I can remember. Oliver was a loner."

"What? The parents are dead?" Max asked.

"I don't think his dad was ever in the picture. His mother was a singer, but I'm sure she died. The police can check it out, but I don't think he had much family.

He used to talk about a sister now and then, but again, nobody close."

"That doesn't mean it's not his father. It's possible. A distant dad who never knew his son, loses it when the kid dies," Max said.

"If he didn't give a shit about Oliver when he was alive, I can't see him caring enough to kill for the bastard now," Ben observed.

"How old was Oliver when he died?" Elijah asked. "Thirty? I might be wrong, but this guy looked around forty, give or take a year. He's too young. It's pushing it for him to be the dad."

"But not impossible," Max exclaimed. "That might explain his absence. If he was a kid himself when Oliver was born. He'd still have that bond."

Daniel sighed. "We're grasping at straws. An ex-boyfriend, a long-lost brother, a distant cousin. It could be any of those things, or none of them. We won't know till they find the bastard. So, what are we supposed to do now? Wait for him to catch up with us? Cause I don't fancy our chances if he does."

"We're leaving tonight," Elijah said. "Moving targets are harder to hit. Ben and I spoke to DI Ritson and he agreed. We should get out of town. The less people who know where we're going the better."

"Where are we going?" Daniel asked.

"I'll tell you when we're on our way. There's less chance of you letting something slip out at the party. Ben's arranged a getaway for him and Max too, and I already had a place arranged for us to go. We'll hit the wrap for an hour and while the party's still swinging, we'll all slip away."

"And the cops? Are they coming with us?"

Elijah shook his head. "Ritson knows where we're going but no one else. We'll be completely on our own. It's better that way."

* * * *

Joe shared a taxi with three of his colleagues in the wardrobe department from the theater to The Majestic Hotel where the wrap party was taking place. Two of them were half cut already, having started on the wine during act one of the evening show. Joe sipped at a bottle of beer in the back of the cab, trying to keep his head together. A little booze would be required for what he had in mind, but he didn't want to spoil it by getting too drunk.

What was going on in Daniel's dressing room just now? The four of them were huddled together like conspirators.

It didn't look like an early start to the party. They were all drinking, but the mood had seemed anything but jovial. Joe knew little of what was going on, with the police and all. He knew the guy they'd found dead on the beach used to be in a band with Daniel, but that was it. There had to be more to it with so many police around. Daniel had kept very tight-lipped about the whole situation.

"Do any of you lot know what went on today?" he asked the rest of his team. "There were a lot more police than usual in the theatre tonight."

The others shook their heads.

"Death threats or something," said Elisa, Max's chief dresser. "No one ever tells us anything."

"I heard there was someone dodgy hanging round the Winter Gardens earlier," offered Stuart, wardrobe assistant to the chorus line.

"Who?"

"I dunno, do I? That's just what people are saying. What does it matter now? The show's over. This lot will be out of our hair tomorrow. They can take their stalkers with them."

The drunken fools found Stuart's comments hilarious. *Arseholes.* Joe was in no mood to laugh. Stuart was right about one thing. Daniel and Elijah would be gone by morning and that would be that. He'd likely never see them again. An unpleasant sensation coiled around his guts. They couldn't go. Not yet.

Not without fucking me.

Why had he left it so late? He could have made a move weeks ago. Sure, neither Daniel nor Elijah had given any suggestion they'd welcome a third person in their bed, but loads of people did it. Grindr was full of couples looking for a bit of threesome fun. They wouldn't refuse him if he offered. No-strings sex with a twenty-year-old. *Who will say no to that?*

Joe took a larger swig of beer. What he really wanted was some one-on-one fun-time with Elijah, but if he had to screw to Daniel to get at his boyfriend, it was hardly a chore. Most of the boys he knew preferred Daniel anyway — he was the more classically handsome of the pair — but not Joe.

Joe was Team Elijah all the way.

The taxi arrived at the hotel and they piled out, laughing. The foyer was jammed with familiar faces as they rushed inside.

"Where's the party?" Elisa squealed, almost falling over. Wine, cheap high heels and marble flooring were a precarious combination.

"Main function room," someone directed. "Keep going past reception, you'll find it."

It wasn't difficult. The stomping dance beats of *Roses and Rainbows* could be heard all the way down the corridor.

"Free bar," Stuart screamed as they raced into the function room.

It was early. Most of the crew were still in the foyer and the room, grandly done out in an art deco style to fit the 1920s theme of *Lady Lynda*, was near empty. Joe's colleagues raced for the bar.

"I'm just going to find the toilet," he said.

No one heard him.

Acting like he every right to be there, Joe entered the elevator in the lobby and went straight for the sixth floor. His heart pounded as he stepped into the corridor.

Oh, God, I'm doing this. I'm really doing this.

From his pocket, he produced the card that would grant him entry to Daniel's suite. Joe had stolen the key from Daniel's jacket while he was on stage. He figured Elijah would have a card of his own so they wouldn't be locked out when they returned. Joe needed to get into the room first to prepare their surprise — him.

He listened at the door before trying it. Silence. *Perfect.* He swiped the card over the sensor and the lock released. It was almost too easy. Joe slipped inside before anyone caught him.

His heart raced, but he'd done it. He was in.

He snapped on the lights.

Holy shit. This place is a palace.

He'd seen rooms like it before, but only on TV. He thought only movie and sports stars lived like this. Not real people. The kind of people he knew. Joe stepped cautiously into the living area. There were sofas, a huge television, lamps, pictures, a bar. He crossed straight to the bar. Now he wanted a drink. A strong one. He treated himself to a vodka and knocked it straight off before pouring another.

Better.

Don't hang about. You don't have much time.

Joe discovered the bedroom, which was nearly as big as the living area. The adjoining bathroom was larger than his bedroom at home. The whole suite was bigger than the flat he shared with his mother, and a hell of a lot nicer.

He wondered how long it would take them to finish up at the theater. Joe assumed they'd come straight here to change before the party. When they did, he'd be more than ready for them. He took off his T-shirt and shoes, followed by his jeans and underwear. From the small bag he'd brought with him, he removed his costume and put it on.

A Union Jack jockstrap with a matching baseball cap, teamed with white socks and trainers. The look was an absolute winner with his followers on Instagram and Twitter. They couldn't get enough of his sweet arse and bulging cock whenever he wore this combo. Joe checked it all out in the bedroom mirror, rearranging his dick for maximum impact in the pouch.

He looked awesome.

Time for one more drink before the lucky couple arrives.

* * * *

"Do you want to go upstairs and change first?" Elijah asked as they arrived at The Majestic.

"No," Daniel said. "Let's keep this short. I'm in no mood to party. They can take me as I am. Half an hour and we're out of there."

Daniel had taken off his stage clothes and makeup at the theater and wore a pair of jeans and chambray shirt. The casual look suited him. Elijah knew he'd be the most desirable man at the party. He slipped a hand around Daniel's waist and led him through the lobby.

"C'mon then, let's get it over with."

Max and Ben's car had arrived a minute before them. A large group of people surrounded her at the entrance to the party, clamoring for attention.

"Guys," she said. "Please. Lady Lynda is desperate for a drink. Let me at the bar and then we'll talk." Max put on a good show. She'd keep up the performance for as long as she had to.

As they entered the party, Elijah noticed the way Daniel switched it on too. The angst of the last hour hidden from sight, he smiled and worked the crowd, embracing the crew who'd become like family over the summer.

"I don't know how they do it," Ben said, stepping up beside Elijah.

He nodded. "That's what makes them stars."

"Wanna get a drink?"

"Just a coke," Elijah said. "I'll be driving through the night once we get out of here. I need the caffeine."

"Be right back." Ben headed for the bar.

Elijah stepped back toward the wall. He didn't want to get drawn into conversation with any of the drunken revelers. This was a party, their party. He would only spoil it considering the mood he was in.

The dance floor was packed with hard bodies and lithe limbs, jiving to the dance beats.

He couldn't help remembering the last night on board the *Atlantic Anthem*, when he'd searched the ship for Anouska. It had been a night just like this. The ship's entertainment crew had been enjoying their end of season party, oblivious to the fact that Anouska, one of their own, was dead. Anouska Frost, the first person to die because of Oliver Gill.

And the last? Not a chance. Oliver was intrinsically linked to what was happening now. Elijah knew that.

He cast his eyes anxiously around the ballroom, looking for Daniel, and spotted him by the bar, posing for photographs. Elijah couldn't let him out of sight. The sooner they were out of here and on their own, the safer he would feel. They couldn't underestimate the risks — or the danger they were in.

Elijah jolted as a hand squeezed him on the bottom.

"Hello, stranger," a familiar voice drawled.

Keeley Rank was dressed to the nines in a puffy cocktail gown that had layers and layers of metallic fabric. It had probably cost a fortune but looked like something straight out of the 1980s. She accessorized the look with an excess of bling. She moved in front of him and brought a champagne glass to her glossy lips.

"Keeley," he said. "I don't need to ask what you're doing here."

Her mouth widened. "It's the closing night of a big show. A West End transfer announced for next year. Max LaFranchi and Daniel Blake both on board for the London run. Why wouldn't I be here for that? I'm not a just a fabulous cook who was criminally robbed of the *Top Cook* trophy. I'm a celebrity journalist, remember?"

"I know exactly what kind of journalist you are," he retorted.

"Now, now, don't be mean. It was naughty of you to rush off without saying a word on Tuesday. We all expected you at *our* wrap party. We didn't know what to think when you didn't turn up. It's a bad show, you know. The winner who snubs his own victory party. I told the producers they should have given the prize to me."

"I had more important places to be."

Keeley rolled her eyes elaborately. "You could have said something. Us being friends and all."

"I'll tell you now exactly what I told you in Edinburgh. You won't get a story from me or Daniel."

She laughed. "This story is bigger than either of you. You don't imagine you can keep it from me. I told you this would be my next book. Only then, I didn't realize how big a book it would be. This story is huge, Elijah. And whether you like it or not, this bitch is all over it."

* * * *

Joe balanced his mobile phone on the back of the toilet cistern and set the timer on the camera to five seconds. As the clock counted down his assumed a pose — bent over, arse raised and cheeks spread, a cocky smile on his face as he looked across his shoulder at the camera. A white flash lit up the room. He checked the image, zooming in to view his silky-smooth butt crack.

Perfect.

He set the timer for another photo.

It was too good an opportunity to miss. This suite, this bathroom, who wouldn't want a bunch of sexy selfies in here? His followers would blow a nut when he uploaded the goods. He was already wearing their favorite costume. The Union Jack jockstrap got an insane reaction whenever he posted pictures of it.

Joe freed his dick from the confines of the pouch and posed for another round of snaps, pouting and leering at the camera.

Maybe Daniel and Elijah would like to film it when they fucked him. That would be unbelievably hot. And having a record of the act too. To relive the encounter again and again. He would ask them, but not straight away. Let them ravage his butt with no distraction first.

Joe adjusted the jockstrap, covering his dick again. He'd have to leave it alone for a while. He'd got himself so turned on, he'd blow a load the second they even looked at him. Not cool. He had to play it far smoother than that if he wanted to impress them.

Joe walked back to the living room. *Might as well take some more selfies while I wait for them. Where are they anyway?* Surely not at the theater. Daniel must be sick of the place. Joe certainly wouldn't hang around that dressing room when he had a suite like this to come back to.

He found a spot to set his camera on a side table and posed for a few more revealing pictures, putting one leg on the sofa to widen his butt. His followers couldn't get enough of his juicy hole. Hopefully Elijah and Daniel would feel the same.

Joe's selfie session was cut short by a noise at the door.

He froze.

Someone tried the handle.

Elijah! This is it. They must have come straight up before realizing they didn't have a key.

Joe's heart sped as he crossed the room. Elijah was about to get a huge surprise.

He experienced a split-second moment of doubt. They might not want him. Might not be interested. Joe swiped the idea away. *Why wouldn't they want me?*

With the bold confidence of youth, he adjusted the cap on his head and opened the door, smiling lasciviously.

"Surprise," he said, before realizing, too late, that the man at the door was not Elijah or Daniel.

He was tall and broad. Kind of sexy in a mean-looking way. Joe had barely registered what the man looked like before he clamped a strong hand over Joe's mouth and barged into the suite.

Chapter Eighteen

It required all of Daniel's skill as an actor to maintain his smile and a veneer of enthusiasm during the party. He wanted out, and soon. It should have been the highlight of the week, a final get-together with all the friends and acquaintances he'd made this summer, but it was more like a torture. A trial of endurance he had to get through.

He plastered a grin on his face and tried not to glaze over as he spoke to people around the room and posed for photographs. He'd already stayed longer than he'd intended. Despite the distraction of people and music, his mind kept wandering back to what had happened to Elijah this afternoon. How close he'd come to losing him. He couldn't stop himself from checking the faces of people attending. There were plenty he didn't know. The party wasn't just for the cast and crew of the show, staff from the theater and the Winter Gardens had been invited too. A select number of press had also been allowed in. There might be three hundred people here and there were certainly more strangers than friends among the crowd.

The man who'd attacked Elijah could be right next to them.

Daniel suspected everyone and studied each face he saw.

Fortyish, Elijah had said about the man. Well-built and a little rough. That hardly narrowed it down. The police were still hanging around but he'd already lost confidence in them. The cops were with Elijah this afternoon. *Some use they turned out to be*. Daniel knew that they were on their own. When the killer came for them, they could only rely on themselves. He'd make damn sure he had Elijah's back when it mattered.

He kept glancing over his shoulder, checking that Elijah was where he'd left him.

He was talking to Ben and a blonde woman near the bar. She looked kind of familiar. Decidedly groomed and well over-the-top.

Bloody hell, it's Keeley Rank. What's she doing here?

Daniel, without giving it much thought, knew the answer to that question. Keeley was a tabloid journalist and celebrity misery was her stock and trade. Of course she'd be here. Blackpool had it all right now. Keeley would be in her element. *She must have pulled a few strings to wangle an invitation. No one would willingly invite her.* And he knew with certainty that Max couldn't stand her. Keeley had once written a profile on her for a Sunday rag. Max had been rebuilding her career after a difficult few years. Instead of focusing on the positive, Keeley had laid bare all of Max's failures — eating disorders, disastrous relationships, flop shows, miscarriages, mental breakdowns.

"That bitch almost got me fired," Max had confided to him earlier in the run, when she'd learned Elijah was competing against Keeley in *Celebrity Top Cook*. "The producers had taken a gamble, casting me in a show after so long away. I was so grateful to them, but Keeley's shitty article damn near ruined everything. They got cold feet after reading the hatchet job she did on me."

Where is Max now? Daniel scanned the party and saw her surrounded by a group of riggers on the far side of the room, oblivious to the poisonous journalist. She looked pretty engaged and he hoped she'd stay there. A catfight between Max and Keeley was not how he wanted this night to end. Thank God, he wouldn't have to stay much longer.

A slender arm linked into his. "Daniel." Rachel Lopez's sweet scent surrounded him as she laid kisses on both his cheeks. "You have been sensational. The best. After everything you've been through this week, to perform the way you did today. I don't think I've directed anyone as professional as you."

Daniel grinned and placed a kiss on Rachel's heavily made-up cheek. As well as perfume, he realized that she also reeked of booze. He hadn't seen the director drunk before. *But hey, if she couldn't get bombed on the last night, when could she?*

"You know, we didn't consider anyone else for this role," Rachel said loudly. Like most drunk people, she'd lost control of her volume. "You were the only one we wanted. But let me tell you." She waggled a bejeweled finger in his face. "You've exceeded everyone's expectations. 'Specally mine. You've been incredible. And I'm so glad you agreed to London. I didn't want to look for someone else to play your part. It's you. Only you. I mean that."

Whoa, he thought, *she really is drunk*. But it was nice of her to say. He always knew he'd been a front runner for the show, but he'd never suspected he was the only runner. After such a shitty year, he appreciated the information. "I'm honoured you thought of me."

"I'm telling you," she said, swaying. "It was only you. C'mon, dance with me." She grabbed his arm, dragging him toward the floor.

He tried to resist. "I'm not in the mood for dancing."

"Rubbish," she bawled, shouldering aside the crowd that had formed around the dancefloor. "You're the leading man. You have to dance. Check your contract."

Daniel reluctantly obliged. It was surely less hassle to do what she wanted than argue. It would be over soon enough. One dance, then he'd be out. He loved these guys, but he needed to be with Elijah tonight. They could enjoy the party without him.

As they made it to the dancefloor the DJ switched records and the dance remix of *Roses and Rainbows* started playing. *How many times does he intend spinning this track tonight?* Daniel had heard it twice already. But it was the impetus needed to kick the party off. In seconds, the floor around them filled with people. Daniel gave in, raising his arms to the thumping track.

Maybe Max would become a disco diva after all. If the popularity of the song translated into the gay clubs, she'd be onto a winner.

One dance, he told himself. *At the end of this record, I'm leaving.*

* * * *

The boy hit the floor in an unconscious heap. Not dead yet, but he soon would be. Sonny would make sure of that. He stepped over the boy to check the rest of the suite. Bedroom, bathroom, both were empty. He returned to the living room. He had no idea who the kid was, but from the way he was dressed he looked pretty comfortable about the place.

Jesus, what is it with these queers? Parading around in underpants with the arse hanging out. Answering the door in the frigging thing. *What is this all about?*

Sonny wondered whether the boy was an escort. More than likely. Daniel and Elijah looking to amuse themselves with a little boy-toy. Well, the slut had found himself in the wrong place at the wrong time. Sonny had had no choice but to knock him out cold, and fast. The hotel was crawling with cops. A single noise complaint from the adjoining rooms and the pigs would come swarming up here. He couldn't have that, not now he was so close. He'd fucked things up with Elijah this afternoon. There could be no more mistakes. Daniel and Elijah had to die tonight.

If he could take out the black guy and the woman too, that would be a bonus, but they were secondary concerns. The queers were his prize.

It suddenly occurred to him that they might have checked out already. He hadn't been watching them all day. Maybe they'd spilt before going to the theater. This little butt boy could have nothing to do with them. Maybe he was the next guest.

Shit. Blood pounded in Sonny's temples, getting louder, more painful.

He'd made too many mistakes already. He was getting too old for this. Too reckless. He wasn't as clever as he thought he was. And one thing he knew from experience – stupid people always got caught.

He clenched his gloved fist into a ball and punched his forehead, once, twice and a third time, much harder. Through gritted teeth he inhaled, bringing his fractured thinking under control. To lose it now would be unforgivable. After a slow count to ten, he regained his composure.

Sonny strode to the bedroom and spied a suitcase in the corner, its lid unfastened. He stooped to inspect it. It was full almost to the top with folded clothes. Expensive shirts, a cashmere jersey. Not the sort of stuff he'd expect that unconscious piece of trash to wear. He searched the exterior of the case, looking for a luggage tag, anything that would identify it as Daniel's. Nothing.

On the dresser he discovered a couple of bottles of aftershave and a bowl full of loose change. They could belong to anybody. He tore into the drawers, still searching. Hotel notepaper, pens, a hair drier, a guide to Blackpool. In the next drawer down, he found a stack of glossy eight-by-six-inch photographs. He snatched the top picture and looked at it. *Yes.* Daniel's publicity photos. The kind of shit he'd sign for sad fans and autograph hunters. They were next to an assortment of silver and gold pens. He would never leave this crap behind.

Sonny breathed easily. Daniel had not checked out.

Stupid to think that he would. What was wrong with him? The pressure getting to be too much? No, he thrived on stress. Murder was a pleasure, not a strain. Maybe he'd made a mistake killing Christian the other night. It had put them on alert and him at a disadvantage. He'd thought it would be fun to be frightened, but bringing the cops to the scene had only complicated things.

He should have waited until tomorrow and hit them at home, when they'd least expect it. But no, he wanted the glory of killing Daniel on the closing night of the show, thinking of the splashy headlines and stories that would dominate the papers on Monday.

Suddenly his cock hardened.

That's more like it. The thrill was back. Now was no time to doubt himself.

Killing Daniel and Elijah, and this boy, whoever he was, would be the greatest kick.

Better than any orgasm.

Better than any woman.

Better than anything.

* * * *

Elijah watched the clock. It had gone one. They should have left by now, but the party was swinging. He saw Daniel across the ballroom. Despite the best intentions, he was trapped. Each time Daniel tried to excuse himself from a group of people, he was collared by another. Everyone wanted a piece of him.

Thankfully Keeley hadn't caught him yet. Elijah saw her on the other side of the dance floor schmoozing the producers, well away from Daniel. He intended to keep it that way. It was time to intervene and get Daniel out of here.

As he drained his coke and made a move across the room, he was intercepted by DI Ritson. The inspector, in his characteristic gray suit, stuck out a mile among the theatrical revelers. "Got a minute?" he asked, gesturing for Elijah to follow him to the foyer, away from the pounding dance music.

A handful of people hung round the lobby. Mainly older, looking for a place to talk away from the music. A uniformed police woman stood station at the main door, next to the concierge.

"When are you leaving?" Ritson asked.

"Soon," Elijah told him.

"I expected you both to be gone by now," the inspector pushed.

Elijah checked his watch again. "And so did I. But Daniel can't just hit-and-run his own party. He's the leading man. People want to say goodbye."

Ritson's mouth twitched downward. "And someone wants to harm him. I don't need to remind you of that, I'm sure."

"Point taken. I was about to bust him out when you caught me. We'll be on our way within the next half an hour."

"Good. Have you spotted anyone who shouldn't be here? Any faces stand out?"

He shook his head. "I don't know anyone beside the main cast. I haven't a clue who should be here or shouldn't. But I haven't seen the guy from this afternoon. Believe me, I've been looking. If I see that bastard again—"

"You'll notify one of my officers," Ritson said firmly. "I want a live suspect, not a dead witness. No risks. Got it?"

Elijah nodded.

"Even if you're not sure. If you only half suspect, or have a gut feeling something is wrong, call for help. Do not challenge the man alone."

"Got it."

"And no one knows where you're heading from here?"

"Not even Daniel," Elijah assured him. "I figured he can't get loose lipped about something he doesn't know."

"Smart. All right, find your fella and get out of here."

Daniel was still ensconced in a crowd when Elijah returned to the party. Two men had their arms around him, while a third snapped photos on his camera. *How many pictures do these guys need?* It seemed like they'd been photographing Daniel from the moment he arrived. Elijah had never achieved that level of celebrity, and based on all this, he hoped he never would.

"Mind if I interrupt?" he asked, barging forward to put a proprietary arm around Daniel and drag him out of the cluster.

Daniel came willingly. "Thanks. My face aches from smiling so much."

"We have to go," Elijah explained. "Inspector's orders. Ritson wants us out."

"There's a couple more people I need to say goodbye to. Alisha and her husband Marcus. I can't go without talking to them. Five minutes, maximum."

"Five minutes in that crowd means twenty," Elijah said. "Look, you talk to who you need to and I'll go up to the room and throw the rest of our stuff in the cases. Meet me there in twenty and we'll hit the road."

Daniel shook his head. "Not after what nearly happened today. You're not going anywhere on your own. You'll have to wait for me."

"The hotel is crawling with police," Elijah told him.

"And they were watching you this afternoon too."

"Point taken," he agreed. Casting his eyes around, he spotted Ben standing by the door, looking bored out of his brain. No doubt waiting for Max to bid her goodbyes too. Perfect. "Listen, I'll take Ben with me. The two of us will deal with the cases, you do what you have to down here and round up Max, then we'll all be on our way in half an hour."

Daniel followed his gaze, seeing Ben on his own. "All right," he said, pulling Elijah closer for a kiss. "You take Ben. I'll grab Max and we'll be right behind you."

Their lips touched again. It was a moment of perfect calm in the craziness of the night.

* * * *

Alisha Cameron knew of Daniel's troubles and didn't object when he told her he had to leave early. He shook the hand of her husband, Marcus, a handsome silver fox with electric-blue eyes. Daniel bet Marcus had been a knockout in his youth. He was still a striking man, with the hair, the eyes, a suntan and an immaculately tailored suit.

Alisha pulled Daniel into a perfumed embraced and planted a soft kiss on his cheek. "Thank you," she said. "For agreeing to London. I didn't want to recast. You and Max *are* the show. We can't do it without you. Now look after yourself. Whatever the hell is going on, I want you in London. As a callous, money-grabbing producer, I'm telling you, you have to stay alive."

Daniel knew the genuine concern behind her joke. As a producer, Alisha cared about everyone in her team. She had a sterling reputation.

"Don't worry," he said, adopting a breezy tone that was the antithesis of how he felt. "It's the London

Palladium. I'll kill anyone who tries to keep me from that stage. That's a promise."

Time to leave. He'd spoken to everyone he felt obliged to and posed for pictures with as many people as he could manage. He was done.

Roses and Rainbows started off again. The DJ had decided to play it after every fifth record and the reaction grew rowdier with each repeat. Cheers of approval ran around the room as people raced to the floor, arms raised, to dance once more.

Daniel cast around for Max, hoping she hadn't been dragged into another dance. They would never get out of here.

"Daniel." A sharp hand gripped his biceps.

"Okay." He sighed. "One quick photo and I really have to go."

Keeley Rank's lips formed a smile, but her eyes were hard and inscrutable. "A *selfie*. Well, if you really must, though I have to confess it's not the kind of thing I usually go in for."

Her nickname was The Dwarf with the Poisoned Pen, but it still surprised Daniel how short she was. She tried to counter it with drag-queen heels and a few inches of lacquered hair, but still came short of Daniel's chest.

"Oh, hello," he said without enthusiasm. *Where is Max?* He hoped she didn't see him with the journalist. She'd have a fit.

"I know we haven't met," Keeley persisted, her eyes staring into his, "but I feel as though I know you so well. Elijah never stopped talking about you. All through the competition it was Daniel this, Daniel that. He never shut up. He's absolutely crazy about you — you know that, of course."

Daniel gave her a practiced smile. "I'm crazy about him. I don't mean to be rude, but I have somewhere else to be. Excuse me."

She tightened the grip on his arm. "I kept telling him what a fan of yours I am."

He could smell the bullshit. "Thanks. Elijah never mentioned it."

"Oh, I'm a fan from way back. I'm old enough to remember Overload. I always thought you boys should have been bigger than you were. You had so much talent. I just loved that ELO cover you did."

He tore his arm away from her. "Empty flattery doesn't work on me."

At last she dropped the sugary smile. "Then I'll cut to the chase. I've been researching what happened to you on the *Atlantic Anthem*. The real story of what went down on that ship was going to be the subject of my next book. Until this week. Now I realize the *Anthem* might only be one chapter in a far bigger story."

"No," he said, holding down his anger.

"No what?"

"I'm not talking to you. About the *Anthem*, Overload or anything else."

"You'd be wise if you did," she persisted. "You see, I'm going to write the book. I've already explained this to Elijah. Whether you cooperate or not, the book will still happen. I'm giving you the opportunity to tell your side first. It would be better for both of you if you did."

"You can write whatever the hell you like," he said, already walking away. "You always do, but I'll be fucked if I have anything to do with it."

* * * *

Ben and Elijah waited for the elevator to arrive. Despite the time, Elijah was wide awake. They had a long drive ahead of them. They wouldn't reach their destination before dawn. He knew he'd be fine. He wouldn't be able to sleep till he got Daniel away from here, to a place of safety. Even then, sleep would not come easily.

Would they ever be safe again? The question bugged him like a fly. The answer was yes — of course they would. This was a moment of crisis. They'd get over it. But doubt remained. He'd thought they were safe once before. That nothing could be as bad as that night at sea. After everything this week, he was no longer sure of anything.

He forced himself to focus on the moment. Right now, all that mattered was getting Daniel out of town, taking him to a place where no one would find them. Safe for the moment — that would be enough.

A middle-aged man and woman sat on a sofa in the front of the lobby. They'd both had far too much to drink and were arguing at full volume, oblivious to their public surroundings.

"You were looking at her tits," the woman screamed at the man, though their faces were inches apart. "You dirty bastard."

"No, I wasn't. I was looking at *your* tits," he slurred back.

"I'm glad they got that settled," Ben said wryly as they stepped into the lift. The argument continued as the doors closed.

"I doubt anything is settled," Elijah said. "They'll be battling for a long time yet." He'd never understood couples who spent all their time tearing at each other's throats. He'd met plenty of people who claimed to be in love but couldn't stand the sight of each other. *How can that be love? When they argue over nothing at all?*

There was enough craziness in the world without spending time with people who were nothing but an irritation. He could do without that kind of love.

"Who shall we pack up first?" Ben asked. "Daniel or Max?"

"Daniel," he said. "I suspect he'll be the easier of the two."

Ben chuckled. "I think you've got the wrong idea about Max. She projects this diva image when she's working, but she's pretty low maintenance out of the spotlight. Quite tomboyish even."

"I bet she still has twice as much luggage as my guy."

"Yeah," Ben agreed. "And then some."

They got out of the lift. Elijah hoped when all this was over, he could stay friends with Ben. He liked him a lot. And things were looking good between him and Max. Now Daniel had committed to work with her again, she would be around for a while. He hoped Ben would be too.

They reached Daniel's suite. Elijah took out his card and unlocked the door. His senses were on high alert and he knew straight away something was wrong.

Then he saw a table lamp knocked on its side and a broken glass.

And on the floor, a figure. A near naked body streaked with blood, not moving.

It was Joe.

Oh, God, not another one.

Then a voice spoke from the corner of the room. Quiet, controlled, it said, "Come in, the pair of you. Hands high where I can see them. First one to make a sound gets a bullet in the kneecap."

Chapter Nineteen

The man had changed clothes since Elijah had seen him last, and no longer wore the glasses, but it was him. The eyes were unmistakable, as cold and predatory as a great white shark.

"I won't warn you again," he said, angling the gun toward Elijah's face. It was some kind of automatic pistol. "Get inside before I change my mind about the knees and go for a more vital target instead."

Elijah had always wondered how he'd feel with a gun pointed at him. A real gun. He was no stranger to the fake things. In a short acting career that had frequently seen him cast as a bad guy, he'd shot and been shot at a dozen times, none of which had prepared him for this. If the man let loose, there'd be no stunt bullets or safety mattress to break his fall. This was cripplingly real.

Bang, bang – you're dead.

"Take it easy," Elijah said, raising his hands in front of him. "We'll do what you want. Don't go crazy."

He walked in ahead of Ben.

"Shut the door," the man ordered.

Elijah scanned the room, trying to get an idea of what the hell had happened. Joe was a heap on the floor. *Is he breathing?* Elijah couldn't tell. The boy was worryingly still. The worst of the blood looked to be coming from his head. *Where are his clothes?*

"What happened to Joe?" he asked, taking a step toward him.

"Stay where you are," the man said in a flat voice, bare of any humanity.

"Just let me see he's all right. He's bleeding."

"I know he's fucking bleeding," the man sneered. "He didn't punch himself out. You'll be bleeding yourself if you don't keep still."

"Who are you?" Ben asked, recovering his voice.

"Enough with the questions, unless you want an answer from my fist." The man's lips curled into a vulgar sneer, revealing perfectly white and even teeth. *Veneers*, Elijah thought, *or a pallet, probably lost his natural teeth fighting.* He had the looks and build of a heavyweight boxer or rugby player, someone who'd been roughed up in his time.

Elijah looked around again, searching for anything that might come in useful. He saw nothing. A couple of table lamps, a silver tray — useless against the firepower of a pistol. The suite had been designed for luxury, not self-defense.

"Where's Daniel Blake?" the man asked.

Elijah froze. Icy fingers tightened around his heart. Daniel. How long before he followed them up and walked straight into this psychopath's trap? "He left already," Elijah said with a conviction he didn't feel.

"Like fuck he did." The man's voice was sinisterly soft.

"He's not coming," Elijah said, injecting greater strength into his words, hoping the man hadn't been watching them. "He left straight from the theatre. The cops insisted he did. There are police all over this hotel. The place is crawling. Whatever you think you're doing, you'll never get away with it."

"This place is crawling with cops and I *still* got in here." The man laughed. "Don't you worry about them. Once again, where's Daniel? And think carefully about your answer. You already know I'm not big on having to ask the same thing twice."

"And I've already told you — he's not here."

The man looked slowly between them before speaking again. "Suit yourself. If Daniel isn't coming, I can still have some fun. I don't know who this slut-boy is, can't say I care much, but the two of you, well, you guys are very much on my hit list."

* * * *

Max had been ambushed by staff from the Winter Gardens. Daniel politely interrupted and guided her away from the group.

"Ready to get going?" he asked. "I think we've done enough."

She nodded. "I'm beat. And if I have to hear that bloody song of mine one more time, I'll scream."

"Anyone else you want to see before we go?"

"No, I think I've spoken to everyone now. Except that bitch" — she pointed to Keeley Rank — "who invited her?"

"I'm sure she invited herself," Daniel said, still seething from the way Keeley had finagled an encounter with him. It was no surprise she wanted to write a book. He'd expected it for a while. Maybe not Keeley, but he'd known someone would come sniffing around for the story. It was too juicy to resist. There'd be even more interest now.

Max linked arms with him. "Come on, let's split. We've done our part. Don't make eye contact and we might get out without being stopped."

They got as far as the door before *Roses and Rainbows* struck up again. Daniel laughed.

"Jesus." Max groaned. "Give it a rest. I can't take anymore."

"That song will follow you around forever more. You realize that?"

"All too clearly. What the hell was I thinking? Disco and show tunes. As if my career wasn't camp enough already."

Despite her objection, he could see how much she loved it. And deserved it. All singers dreamed of having a hit record and all the early indications were that this would be a smash, camp or not.

The heady thrum of music leaked out into the foyer.

Daniel was relieved to reach the hotel lobby. They'd finally made it out of the party. His responsibility to *Lady Lynda* was done. Now he wanted to get away and spend some quiet, quality time with Elijah. In half an hour, they'd be out of the hotel and on their way to wherever Elijah had in mind. Daniel didn't care where they headed, as long as they were together.

He needed to escape the madness, if only for a few days. They'd be back for Christian's funeral soon enough. Until then, he needed time with Elijah to de-stress.

A few guests from the party had spilled into the lobby, but no one paid them any attention. A middle-aged couple who he didn't recognize were on their feet arguing in the center of the lounge.

"You're an arsehole," the woman screamed at the man. "My sister told me not to marry you, and she was right."

"Your sister's a miserable bitch, the same as you," the man replied, so drunk that all his words merged into one.

"A typical Saturday night in Blackpool," Max deadpanned as they passed.

Daniel found he was quickly going off the place, all the excesses and eccentricities that came with it. Blackpool wasn't called the Vegas of the north for nothing. With so much alcohol consumed, often from breakfast onward, it wasn't unusual for people to get lively toward the end of the night. It was part of the fun. But the violence this week had tainted it for him. Previously, he might have laughed at a drunken couple having an outlandish argument in public. Not now. Not anymore.

"I'm glad we're leaving," he said, and meant it, hitting the button for the elevator.

Right then, the woman spat in the face of her husband.

"You little bitch," he sneered, raising his hand.

One of the riggers from the show, a huge guy called Phil, stepped in before the man could strike.

"No man should ever hit a lady," Phil said.

"No," the husband snarled, "but a nosy fucker like you deserves it every time." His balled fist and struck Phil's solid belly.

The wife flung herself at Phil's head, clawed fingers going for his eyes. Suddenly there were half a dozen people involved as supporters for either side of the argument joined in. Daniel saw an explosion of blood as a fist connected with someone's nose.

The cops stationed at the hotel entrance hurried to break it up.

"Oh, lord," Max cried as it rapidly descended into a riot.

The elevator arrived. Daniel caught her shoulder and hurried her inside.

* * * *

Keeping the gun trained on them both, Sonny ordered Ben to fasten Elijah's hands behind his back with a silk tie he'd found in one of the open suitcases.

"Tight," he warned. "Any slack in the binds and I'll take it out on both of you. Then I won't be so kind to Daniel and the woman."

"Why are you doing this?" Ben asked, looking at Sonny across Elijah's shoulder while getting busy with the fastenings. "I don't know who the hell you are. Never seen you before in my life, man. There's no reason for any of it."

Sonny liked to see the fear in their eyes. With Christian, he'd been denied that, forced to work quickly. Not this time. He might not have all night — the hotel *was* crawling with police — but he'd have the pleasure of making them suffer before he was done.

"There's a reason," Sonny snarled. "And you're right about one thing, you don't know me."

"So why?"

"It's personal."

"For who?"

He laughed. "Not me. I'm just doing a friend a favour."

"What the fuck?" Elijah cried. "What kind of lunatic are you?"

"Now that, Mister Mann, is the first sensible question you've asked. What kind of lunatic am I? Well, I guess I'm not the best person to answer that, am I? Slut-boy here, he knows, but he's not talking anymore. And your other fella Christian, he certainly knew, but he's not talking either. So now, I guess you two will find out for yourselves."

The look of fear in their eyes was really something.

Sonny checked the fastening around Elijah's wrists, pleased to see it held. Ben hadn't tried to fool him with a loose knot. He shoved Elijah's face against the wall, then bound Ben's hands behind his back. When they were both secure, he dragged them into the middle of the room and down on their knees.

Rooting through the suitcase, he found a dirty pair of socks and another tie. Exactly what he needed. Sonny grabbed a fistful of Elijah's hair and tore back his head until his mouth opened. Quickly, he shoved the sock inside, pushing it to the back of his throat. Elijah struggled, shaking his head, but it was too late. Sonny wedged the bundle deep and wrapped the tie around Elijah's mouth to make an improvised but effective gag.

"Now," he said. "Elijah being Daniel's boyfriend and all, I don't expect him to give the guy up, no matter how much I try to persuade him otherwise. But I've got a feeling I might fare better with you."

He stood, enjoying the frightened look on their faces, the panic in their eyes. He slowly crossed the room, giving them time to digest the gravity of their situation. From the jacket he'd left over the sofa, he removed his knife. The blade he'd used to kill Christian. He raised it slowly so they could both see, turning it to catch the light.

The fear in their eyes rose a hundredfold.

Sonny beamed. A gun was a handy tool to control people. They would always obey the man with the shooter. But nothing inspired terror like a cutter.

He knelt in front of Elijah. His dark eyes were wet with tears. The dilated pupils looked like pools of oil in the softly lit living room. The cold glint of his blade reflected in their surface. He turned his gaze to Ben.

"So," he said. "Why don't we try this again? From the top. Where's Daniel Blake?"

Ben inhaled a ragged breath. "I...don't know."

Sonny let the answer linger. A beat. Two beats.

"I don't think you understand the way this works," he said at last.

"Don't," Ben pleaded. "No."

Elijah's dark eyes widened further.

That was the part Sonny loved best. When they knew what was coming but still didn't believe.

With one smooth lunge, he slid the knife into Elijah's lower abdomen, and as he screamed against the bundle in his mouth, Sonny twisted it.

* * * *

Joe regained consciousness to the sound of muffled screaming. His head hurt, the kind of pain he'd never known the like of. He wanted to cry—it blazed like a fire in the center if his forehead. But an inherently deep instinct for survival made him bury the sound.

Don't move, he warned himself, *not the slightest twinge.* His life depended on it.

He breathed shallowly, afraid even that would give him away, and willed the pain to come under control.

He was cold. As he lay there, dazzled, straining to remember where he was, what had gone down, there was another muffled scream.

And a man's voice cried, "Stop."

Joe noticed something in the tone of the scream. A familiar timbre. Then his memory returned in vivid detail. *The hotel. Daniel and Elijah's suite. The strange man.*

Oh, God. What the hell is happening?

Slowly, Joe opened his eyes a crack, then wider, blinking something wet from his lids. Blood.

He was in the corner of the living room, against the wall. A man — *the man* — had his back to him, occupied with someone else in front of him. The screams came from that direction. Joe raised his head a fraction from the floor.

Fuck, it's Elijah. He knelt before the stranger, bound and gagged. A dark red patch stained his T-shirt, growing wider. The psycho had stabbed him.

"Where's Daniel?" the man asked calmly.

"I don't fucking know," someone else answered. *Ben. It's Ben. Also tied up. What's going on?*

A nightmare. A living nightmare. But the pain in his head proved how real the situation was.

The man's shoulder gave a jerk. Another muffled scream from Elijah as the blade struck home.

Joe had to do something. Elijah and Ben were tied up. He was the only one free. The only one who stood a chance. But what? He could never take on that big guy, even without the knife.

Joe's phone lay feet away, within easy reach. He couldn't make a call, not without the man hearing, and that wouldn't help any of them. But he had to do something.

The phone was all he had.

Slowly, cautiously, Joe reached for the handset.

* * * *

"I hate to see people arguing like that," Max said in the elevator. "Why stay with someone if you can't bear the sight of them? It's stupid. And fighting…for fuck's sake, it's like something from the old west."

"I totally agree," Daniel said. "After a great run this summer, everything seems to have turned to shit this week. The show might have ended on a high, but nothing else has."

Max came closer and put her arm around him. "You'll get over it and be better for it. I once did a concert tour in the middle of a full-on mental breakdown, and I never missed a show. The audience didn't have a clue there was anything wrong. I gave them my soul every single night. Hitting the big notes and telling jokes. It was all teeth, tits and sparkle on stage. The morning after the tour ended I checked into a hospital for six weeks. You're a trooper, just like me. You'll always go on with the show."

He hugged her back. "Thanks for the vote of confidence. I don't want to think about another show. I just want out of this hotel and then to sleep for thirty-six hours straight."

"I'm right with you there." She stooped to unfasten her shoes and take them off. "And I don't want sex until at least Tuesday."

Daniel laughed. "I might hold off till Monday."

"Knowing you and Elijah like I do, I don't think you'll hold out till morning, never mind Monday."

As the elevator came to a stop, Daniel's phone vibrated in his pocket. Probably Elijah, telling him to hurry up. He glanced quickly at the screen. The caller ID read Joe Elliott. A video call.

Daniel knew in a second that something was wrong. Joe had no reason to call him tonight. He hit answer, fearing the worst.

The screen went blank and buffered, taking an age for the image to appear. Max, seeming to sense the change in Daniel's mood, crowded close to look at the display.

"What is it?" she whispered.

"I don't know."

At last the picture loaded, blurred and shaky, before coming into focus. Daniel stared at the image, seeking to make sense of the unfamiliar angle. Joe looked to be filming this from the floor. As Daniel's eyes adjusted, he understood what he was looking at.

His hotel suite shot from the corner of the room. There were three figures in the frame. One man had his back to the camera. Daniel couldn't see who he was, but Ben and Elijah knelt in front of him. *Oh, shit.* Elijah was bleeding. There was blood everywhere.

"Oh, my God," screamed Max. "Is that happening now?"

Daniel thought quickly. "It's a live stream. It means they're alive. For now. We don't have time to waste."

The impulse to panic was overridden by a stronger, more controlled instinct. Elijah was in danger—if Daniel was going to save him, he couldn't lose his shit. They had to move fast.

"Go back to the lobby," he said, thrusting the phone at her. "Show this to the police and get them up here straight away."

She took the phone in trembling hands. "What about you?"

"I'm going in."

"You can't."

"I have to. There's nothing else to do. I'll stall him for as long as I can. To stop him hurting Elijah until the cops get here. Go on, go. Move," he shouted.

Tears ran down Max's face as the elevator doors slid shut.

Daniel turned to the suite and patted his trousers for his key card. It wasn't there. He checked his jacket, his wallet. Nothing.

Shit! He must have dropped it. It could be anywhere between here and the theater. No time to search for it. Elijah needed him now.

Whatever that bastard was doing to him, Daniel would make him pay for it.

Stepping up to the door, he took a deep, calming breath. His whole world was in chaos again. Only he could put it right.

He raised his fist and knocked hard, praying it wouldn't be the last thing he ever did.

Chapter Twenty

Daniel waited. No answer. He put his ear to the door and listened but heard nothing from inside. Fear consumed him, not for himself but for Elijah. What he'd seen on his phone looked bad. Daniel wouldn't lose him. Not a chance.

He pounded on the door, harder this time. He had no plan other than to stall for time. Delay this psycho till Max brought the police up. He would rely entirely on instinct. Whatever he had to do, he'd do it. If he had to sacrifice himself to save Elijah, he's do it in a heartbeat.

"It's Daniel," he shouted.

At last, he heard footsteps on the other side and the click of a lock. The door opened.

Daniel expected some kind of recognition. That he would know the man responsible for the horror, and he would finally understand what it had all been about. But the man was a stranger.

He was around forty with short, graying hair. Too young to be Oliver's father. *Who, then? An older brother?*

An uncle? Daniel searched his face for a family resemblance and saw none.

The man raised a gun and pointed it directly at Daniel's face.

"Inside," he ordered.

"Who are you?" Daniel said, raising his hands and doing what the man wanted. He saw Elijah across the living room. The amount of blood staining his T-shirt was worse than Daniel expected. He rushed toward Elijah.

Daniel was halfway across the room when the man's foot delivered a sharp kick to the back of his knee. Unbalanced, Daniel fell hard, catching the side of his face on the corner of the coffee table, missing his eyes by a fraction. Undeterred, Daniel rose to his hands and knees, straining toward Elijah.

The man's foot connected with the soft flesh of Daniel's belly. He rolled onto his back, struggling to draw breath, clutching his stomach. The man stood over him, casually pointing the gun at Daniel's head.

"Stay," the man said coolly. The suggestion of a smile played across his mouth. The sadistic pleasure spoiled an otherwise handsome face. Daniel stared at him, searching his memory, sure he would find him, but there was nothing.

He didn't believe they'd fallen victim to a random stalker. The murders of Christian and Luke, now this. It was all too personal.

"I don't know you," Daniel said at last.

The man nodded. "That's right. You don't. But I know all about you. It's my business to know."

Daniel should have been afraid but he was consumed by anger. The man had killed his friends, assaulted

Elijah, and all he did was gloat, proud of what he'd done.

"So who are you?"

"You should be more concerned about what I'm going to do, rather than who I am."

"You're a big man with a fucking gun. Big deal. All I see is an inadequate fuck." Daniel growled angrily.

"Daniel," Ben warned. "Don't antagonize him."

Daniel laughed hollowly. "It's a bit late for that. I want to know what this sick bastard is getting out of it. Two people are dead already. There's got to be a reason. A good one at that. Tell me there's a reason, you fucking arsehole."

The man stared at Daniel with an unwavering gaze. "There's always a reason. Always an agenda. But my motivation is simpler than most. I enjoy what I do."

"Bullshit," Daniel spat.

"Bullshit, is it?" the man smiled coldly. He crouched lower, trailing the barrel of his gun across Daniel's chest, moving it downward, he pushed the tip of the weapon into his navel. When he spoke again, his voice was barely more than a whisper. "When I stuck my knife into your boyfriend's guts, oh man, I really enjoyed that." He jabbed the gun into Daniel's abdomen. "All that hot blood gushing over my knuckles. Hearing him scream. That's icing on the cake to me."

"Elijah had nothing to do with Overload, you idiot. He was never in the band," Daniel said.

"I know that." The man laughed. "I always thought the Overload connection was over the top. An unnecessary extravagance. Fun, though. I'll admit that much. I have enjoyed myself. Most boy bands deserve a similar fate, in my opinion, but you boys were special.

But this didn't have much to do with Overload. Not really. The reason your friends are dead, and your boyfriend is spilling his guts over this fine carpet, is you, Daniel. This is all because of you."

* * * *

The lift took an inordinately long time to go back down. Max stabbed at the control panel, hoping it would hurry the damn thing up. Her entire body trembled. She had never experienced fear like this, but she knew she had to keep it together. People were relying on her. Daniel, Elijah, Ben. *Oh, God, Ben, please keep him safe.*

They had only just met. She couldn't lose him already.

Max glanced at the phone again. Poor Joe was still recording, Whatever the hell was happening up there, the boy hadn't been discovered. Not yet.

It was difficult to make out what was going on. She thought she'd seen a gun, briefly, before the man stooped over Daniel. Now all she could see was the back of his shoulders. *The crazy bastard.* Whoever this guy was, he'd proved how dangerous he could be.

Max had firsthand experience of stalkers and how unpredictable they were. In the late 1980s, a woman from Aberdeen used to follow her all over the country. Harmless enough to begin with, attending concerts and appearing at the stage door with homemade presents. Her behavior had soon deteriorated. The woman had poisoned Max's beloved pet dog and broken into the family home — thankfully everyone was out at the time. The dangerousness of some people couldn't be underestimated.

This guy was clearly off-the-scale nuts.

Finally, the elevator reached the lobby.

"Oh, no," Max groaned as the doors opened.

The argument between the drunk couple had descended into a near riot. Max couldn't count the number of people involved, just a mass of tumbling limbs and punches. Broken glass littered the floor. Furniture lay upended. Three police officers struggled to bring a huge man to the floor. He writhed and kicked as they tried to control him.

Max ducked as a glass flew past, shattering against the rear of the lift. Fragments came down in her hair and the back of her clothes. This was complete madness.

She fought the impulse to close the doors. She needed help. She couldn't deal with the situation upstairs on her own.

The cops in the lobby were all tied up with warring drunks. None of that mattered. Her friends were in greater jeopardy than any of these losers.

"I need help," she shouted at the closest police officer. "Please do something."

The officer had a woman in handcuffs and was trying to maneuver her toward the front door. The woman resisted and screamed her protest all the way.

"Get your fucking hands off me, you black cunt," the woman wailed.

The stupid bitch. There are more important things going on than this.

Max ran toward another officer, a burly man with blood streaked down his face. She didn't think the blood was his.

"Please, help," Max begged. "Upstairs. There's a problem upstairs."

The officer pushed straight past her. "You might not have noticed, but we've got a few problems of our own down here."

"It's Daniel Blake," she cried, but it was too late. No one would listen. With tears of frustration blurring her eyes, Max hurried toward the ballroom.

* * * *

Elijah's dizziness grew so great that he realized he must have blacked out. For how long, he didn't know. The pain below was so intense, his body must be shutting down. He'd never felt so weak.

He fought with everything he had, forcing himself awake. He heard voices. Daniel and the man. Elijah groaned and struggled against his bonds. The explosion of pain ripped through his body, threatening him with blackness again. He would not succumb.

"Don't move," said a voice close by. "You'll make the bleeding worse."

Ben. Elijah tried to look at him but could not focus. All he could see was a vague shape in the direction his voice came from.

Daniel. Where is Daniel? Elijah could hear him speaking. His voice was strained. Far different from how he should sound.

"If this is all because of me," Daniel said, "then let everyone else go. You don't need them. Do what you want to me, just spare them please."

No, Daniel. No. You shouldn't be here.

The man, that sick piece of shit, laughed. "Not a chance. You've got to suffer. That's a promise I made. Watching the people you care about die, that was all part of the plan."

What's he talking about? They were living through the final reel of a horror film, brought to ghastly life. *Who is this man? A paid hitman? A vengeful relative?*

"You'll never got out of here," Daniel said. "The cops are downstairs. You can't get out."

"You and your boyfriend seem to hold the police in high regard. They're plods. Undertrained and underpaid pigs. I came in beneath their noses and I'll go out the same way. Now, let's see what we can do about you. It's payback time. And you owe your life."

The man's calmness frightened Daniel. There was no way to unsettle him. There had been little variation in the tone of his voice all through this ordeal. He doubted his heart rate had even increased. He was a professional, all right. A professional killer.

This is all for someone else's benefit. The idea terrified him. That someone would send a hitman after him. But who and why were questions that could wait. All that mattered now was staying alive.

Where are the damn cops? How long since Max left? It seemed like hours.

Elijah groaned. He was still alive. But maybe not for long, looking at him now. His skin had already taken on an ashen pallor. He had lost too much blood.

The man, sensing Daniel's interest in that direction, looked at Elijah. "Time is running out," he said flatly. "Better get on with it."

"Leave him alone," Daniel said.

The man straightened up, kicking Daniel in the belly again.

Daniel doubled over, watching as the man tucked the gun into his waistband and picked up a knife from the side of the sofa. Daniel looked around, searching for something — anything — that would make an effective weapon. He saw nothing.

The man stepped over to Elijah, who was still conscious — barely. Elijah's eyes were trained in Daniel's direction, but he doubted he could see him. His entire expression was unfocused. The look on Elijah's face would haunt him forever. He couldn't lose him now.

"Wait," Daniel shouted. Every second he could stall would buy Elijah precious time. "I have to know why? If you're doing this for someone else, who is it? Who are you working for?"

The man shook his head. "Confidential." The hand holding the knife had developed a twitch.

"If not who, then tell me why?" Daniel said desperately. "Why do so many people have to die? Aren't I enough?"

"Jesus," the man said, showing the first sign of impatience. "What does it matter? You're all on your way out. Asking questions won't change a thing. You'll still die. Your boyfriend will die. Your friends will die. Stall as much as you want but I will still kill you. Got that, you stupid prick?"

C'mon. Where are the fucking cops? We'll all be dead if they don't hurry up.

The man's gaze returned to Elijah. He raised the knife.

"Oliver Gill," Daniel yelled.

The man stiffened.

Daniel pressed home the advantage. "I'm right, aren't I? You're doing this for Oliver. So, what are you? Uncle, brother, ex-lover?"

"I'm no faggot," the man growled. "Not like the rest of you fairies. Now, just to shut you the fuck up, I'm going to say yes—you're right about the first part. Okay. We're done. This ends now."

The man crouched and grabbed a handful of Elijah's hair, exposing his neck. The point of his blade moving toward the target.

The sequence of events lasted only seconds, but Daniel lived every one in minute detail.

The knife connected with Elijah's throat, pressing into the flesh.

Daniel launched from the floor, arms outstretched, already aware that he was too late.

A blur of movement across the man's shoulders. Joe had crawled unseen across the floor and picked up one of the Tiffany lamps. He smashed the heavy base against the back of the man's skull with enough force to make him drop the knife.

The man spun—the reactions of a fighter, a killer. His fist impacted with Joe's jaw. Daniel caught the sound of breaking bone as Joe's near-naked body thudded to the floor. Joe was out of it, but his actions had bought Daniel the time he needed. He leapt across the floor, searching for the fallen knife.

Where did it go?

"Daniel," Ben cried. "His gun."

The man snatched the pistol from his waist band and raised it in infinitely slow motion.

With the skill and agility his dance training had afforded him, Daniel high-kicked. His foot struck the man's gun hand.

The weapon went off as it flew from his grip, the noise was amplified and deafening in the confided space. Daniel didn't see where it had gone, but it was beyond the reach of them both.

The man did not need a weapon to kill. He came down on Daniel with his full weight, pressing him into the floor. His hands were at Daniel's neck.

Powerful thumbs dug into his windpipe.

"As long as you die, I'll be happy," the man snarled, spitting in Daniel's face.

Daniel clawed at his hands, but the grip was unbreakable.

He heard a distant sound of banging. It could be the police at the door, or just the thunder of his own blood in his head.

The grip on his throat tightened.

The man's face, just inches away, became blurred and dark.

Almost gone.

Then a sound, exactly like a gunshot, followed by an explosion, hot and wet, splattering him in the face.

The hands around his throat loosened their deadly grip as the body on top became a dead weight.

Daniel gasped for breath and tasted something bitter — blood. The man was dead. He shoved and dislodged the body, crawling out from under the heap. Where once a hateful face belonged, there was now a pulpy mess. Daniel felt no sorrow or revulsion. Only one thing mattered.

He crawled to Elijah, who was still on his knees, chin slumped on his chest. His entire lower body was drenched in dark blood.

"Elijah," he cried. "Darling."

At the sound of his voice, Elijah made a gurgling sound in his throat. His mouth twitched.

He's alive. Thank God, he's alive.

"Call an ambulance," Daniel screamed at the police officers now flooding the room. "Now."

Chapter Twenty-One

Two days later, Monday afternoon, Daniel sat in the hospital coffee shop with Max, Ben and Detective Inspector Ritson. Daniel hadn't left the hospital for more than a couple of hours. His own injuries had been minor, requiring little more than an examination and a dose of painkillers. Elijah's condition was far more serious. After major surgery on his abdomen that had kept him in theater for most of Saturday, he remained under heavy sedation. Daniel had only left his room to shower and change, and now for this meeting with Ritson, who claimed to have some of the answers.

"This is strictly between the four of us and off the record," Ritson said gravely.

They gathered around a small coffee table on two leather sofas in the corner of the café, away from any of the other patrons. A pair of uniformed constables stood at the entrance. An additional two were on guard outside Elijah's bedroom. Daniel wouldn't have left him otherwise.

"Tell us what you know," Daniel prompted.

Ritson glanced around once more, checking they were not being listened to. "We've identified the man who attacked you as Sonny Rock. Have any of you heard of him?"

They shook their heads.

"Who is the bastard?" Max asked.

"He's got a record," Ritson continued. "He was forty-one. Originally from South Wales, but he's lived all over the UK. The third of four brothers, working-class types with criminal connections, though none of the others have records as long as Sonny. He was in and out of Young Offender Institutions during his teens before getting married at seventeen. His wife was part of a larger criminal family and they put him to work as a bit of muscle. He seriously assaulted a social worker, which led to jail and divorce."

"What's the connection to Oliver? Or any of us?" Daniel asked.

"Let him finish," Max said, putting her hand gently on top of his. Max and Ben had been at the hospital almost as much as he had. They'd left for a few hours on Sunday night to move theirs and Daniel's stuff out of The Majestic and into another hotel. No way could any of them go back there.

"Sonny worked as a bouncer, debt collector and enforcer with four major spells in prison, always for violent offences. He was a sadist who got off on hurting people. Birmingham police questioned him about the murder of a prostitute in 2011, but there was not enough evidence to charge him. That case has never been solved."

"Shit," Max said. She looked from Ben to Daniel, tears brimming in her eyes. "You guys were so close to being dead."

Ben put his arm around her, pulling her into his shoulder. He gently kissed the top of her head. "We're not dead."

"But you could be." She wept.

"What about Oliver?" Daniel insisted. "Is there anything to connect Sonny to him? Or even Overload?"

"We've established nothing yet," Ritson said.

Daniel swore. The mystery was as dense as ever.

"Sonny said more than once that he was doing this on behalf of someone else," Ben pointed out. "And you say he's had gangland connections his entire life. Maybe he was just a hired hand."

"That's one theory we're working on," Ritson remarked. "Among others."

"But hired by who?" Daniel pressed. It infuriated him that they were no nearer to knowing who'd pulled Sonny's strings. "And for what? To murder upward of six people. Who'd be rich enough for that? Who'd be mad enough?"

"Sonny was mad enough," Ritson said. "And a man like that wouldn't require huge amounts of money. He would kill you for the thrill of it."

"Have you connected him to Luke's murder?" Daniel asked.

"The police in Bournemouth are sure they can place him in the area at the time. I'm just waiting for confirmation of that. We're certain it was him."

"Just not who hired the bastard," Daniel said angrily.

* * * *

Joe Elliott was unrecognizable. Propped in his hospital bed on a stack of pillows, the boy was a bruised and battered mess. His head was covered in a swath of bandages, wrapped tight to support his broken jaw. The window of flesh exposed from his eyes to his mouth was tainted with mottled shades of blue and purple. The right eye was swollen shut.

Barely a trace of his good-looks remained. The doctors said he would get better. All he needed was time. The fractures would heal and the bruises would fade, but Daniel knew better than anyone that the emotional damage would last way longer than any physical injuries. Psychological scars were something they would all have to deal with.

Joe's left eye opened slowly as Daniel entered the room. He didn't want to disturb him, just check how he was doing.

"Hi," Joe said. The sound came from the back of his throat as he tried to speak without moving his jaw.

"Don't talk," Daniel said, approaching the bed.

A rush of sadness went through him, looking down at the small, broken body.

"How's Elijah?" Joe croaked.

"The same," Daniel said, holding his hand. "The doctors say he's stable, so that's the best he can be for now."

No one knew what Joe had been doing in his suite on Saturday. He hadn't been well enough to give a full statement to the police yet. Daniel had a good idea of what might have happened but wouldn't embarrass him about it now. He owed Joe his life. Elijah's too.

He'd known for weeks that Joe had a crush on Elijah. Probably more than that. To call it a crush trivialized the strength of Joe's emotions. There'd been jokes about it all over the theater. Daniel had even ribbed Elijah about it a few days ago.

He suspected Joe was responsible for his missing key card. He could have taken it during one of the shows on Saturday. Joe had probably been hurting that day, worried he might never see Elijah again.

It was pure speculation, but Daniel believed Joe had let himself into the suite intending to seduce Elijah, maybe both of them. It hardly mattered, what he had intended. Not anymore.

If he hadn't done what he did, they would all be dead. Elijah, Ben, himself, probably Max too.

Daniel gently squeezed his hand. "You're a hero. It might not feel that way now, but you certainly are."

A large tear rolled over the brim of Joe's good eye and trickled down his purple cheek.

The cops who'd broken into the suite had been unarmed. It had been Joe, thinking fast, who'd found Sonny's gun and blown the sick bastard's head off.

Ritson had told Daniel that the Crown Prosecution Service wanted to charge the boy with murder, manslaughter at best.

'It'll never stick,' Daniel had argued with the DI. *'No jury will convict him for what he did. And I'll spend every penny I own on his defense. That boy won't spend a second in prison.'*

Ritson had shrugged. *'It's out of my hands. CPS make the call on who we charge. For what it's worth, I agree with you, but until Joe tells us what he was doing there, I can't do anything.'*

Sonny Rock was not the kind of man to grass on his criminal connections. If Joe hadn't killed him and Ritson had arrested him instead, he wouldn't have given up his paymaster. They'd be no farther forward.

Daniel was glad he was dead.

"Hang in there, Joe," he said, putting a kiss on his hand. "Whatever happens, I'll look after you. That's a promise."

* * * *

Half an hour later, Daniel sat quietly at another bedside. Elijah had been heavily sedated since coming out of surgery on Sunday night. A canopy had been erected across the center of the bed, keeping the covers clear of his sensitive midsection. Tubes ran from cannulas in both his arms, hooking him to several clear drips and a blood transfusion. A catheter tube led from the covers to a collection bag at the side of the bed.

Daniel watched him sleep. So deeply he was afraid Elijah might never wake up again. An oxygen mask covered his mouth and nose.

Elijah. His man. The person who'd been everything to him for the last year. The strong one who'd held the world at bay while Daniel dealt with his own recovery.

Now Elijah was in a far worse position than Daniel had ever been.

The last forty-eight hours had been the longest of Daniel's life. The ten hours Elijah had spent in surgery had been pure torment. Daniel had come so close to losing him.

He wiped a tear away and took Elijah's hand. He did not respond. *Sleep softly, my darling, you need it.*

Elijah's parents had rushed here yesterday morning with his brother. They had stayed by Daniel during the long hours of surgery and sat with him at Elijah's bedside during the night. His brother had taken them to a hotel that morning to get some sleep and freshen up. They would be back soon.

For now, it was just the two of them. Daniel didn't want it any other way.

When Elijah pulled through this, no one would ever come between them again.

Daniel Blake and Elijah Mann—they'd be stronger than ever.

Elijah groaned in his sleep. His brow furrowed for a couple of seconds, but he didn't open his eyes. Whatever troubled him passed, and he slept calmly again.

"No nightmares," Daniel whispered. "I'm right here. No one can hurt you."

Elijah slept.

After a while, Daniel stood and stepped outside.

"I'll be right back," he told the cops at the door. "Don't leave him."

At the end of the corridor, out of earshot, he took out his phone.

Keeley Rank answered straight away. "Daniel, how is everyone?"

"I don't have time for pleasantries," he told her. "This book of yours. You have a reputation for painstaking research, for getting to the truth, however deeply it's buried."

"Always," she said.

"I'll help you write it on one condition."

"Name it."

"Oliver Gill. I want everything there is to know about that bastard. Where he's from. His family. Everything he did from the moment he was born to the second he jumped into the ocean. I want it all."

"You've got it."

"Then count me in."

Daniel hung up and walked back to the ward. He would find out about Oliver and who'd given the word for Sonny Rock to kill.

When he did, that person would pay dearly.

But right now, Elijah needed him more. Daniel returned to his side. The only place he wanted to be.

Want to see more from this author?
Here's a taster for you to enjoy!

The Coach
Thom Collins

Excerpt

"Why me?" I grumbled. "I know nothing about rugby."

Anna Madley, editor of *The Woodbridge Echo*, didn't take excuses, not from anyone. "You wrote that article on the Durham Cricket team, didn't you? You claimed to know nothing about that when you started."

"But rugby!"

"You're a journalist, Josh. What you don't know, you find out. Do your research. *That's your job.*" Pushing her glasses onto the bridge of her nose, she turned her attention to the computer monitor. The conversation was over. Matter dismissed.

With gritted teeth, I left her office, returning to the icy room I shared with the paper's other two reporters. The only window was an opaque rectangle set high on the wall, which allowed minimal daylight into the poky space. The room was poorly lit by two florescent strips and scant warmth came from a single-bar electric heater. It was mid-February and the room was freezing.

Dixie Ellis wore fingerless gloves as she tapped away at her keyboard with her bright red hair piled beneath a fur-trimmed hat.

"What did you get?" she asked, wrapping her fingers round a mug.

"Local rugby team. They've won a county championship and qualified for a national cup." I sank heavily into my chair. "I hate sports stories. Why couldn't she give it to Kenny? He always does sport. He loves that crap."

"Kenny's on court duty this week."

"Has he left already?"

She nodded.

Bugger. That threw any chance of a swap to the wind.

I clicked off my screen saver and ran a Google search on the Woodbridge Warriors.

I'm a realist and knew that working on the local paper would never lead to a world-grabbing headline, but even in Woodbridge there were more compelling stories than the rugby team progressing through a competition. Dixie was following a spate of home burglaries at the upper end of town, and a pub fight on Saturday night which had turned into a near riot. I doubted our readers had much interest in the rugby win either. Woodbridge was a football town. Any other sport was redundant.

Still, this had to be better than the *Missing Cat Comes Home* headline I'd turned in for last week's edition. I've got nothing against cats but for a journalist it was a career low.

The club didn't have a website, but I found the number for their training ground in the local listings. I dialed straight away. It rang. And rang. And rang.

A man answered just as I was about to give up.

"Hello, Woodbridge Warriors. Leo Mitchell."

"Hi. This is Josh Holleran from *The Woodbridge Echo*. I understand you guys got through to the…er, nationals. You're big news. We'd like to run a report in this week's edition. Maybe even front page. Would it be possible to come along to the ground? Perhaps interview a couple of players, get some pictures."

"A piece in the *Echo* would be wonderful." He sounded excited. "Only there's hardly anyone here right now. I'm the club secretary. Our team is made up of amateurs. They've got jobs away from the pitch. There's a training session on Wednesday night. All the guys will be together then. Could you maybe get along for that?"

"Here's the thing. The paper comes out Thursday, so I need to file my story Wednesday morning at the latest. Is there *anyone* I could speak to today? I'd only require a couple of guys for a picture at the ground, then we could run it with an official photo of the whole team."

"That's a shame," Leo said slowly. "How about this afternoon? I'll make a few calls, see who I can get together. It won't be much, like I say, these lads have jobs. Maybe just the coach and a player."

"That'll be perfect. Say three o'clock?" Appointment agreed, I hung up.

Dixie had left her desk to warm her fingers over the heater. She threw a look across her shoulder. "Rugby has one thing going for it, you know. Some of those boys are stacked. Have you seen the team? Brick shithouses, the lot of them. My kind of men."

I laughed. "I'm not that lucky. They're all at work. I'll call it a triumph if I meet a single player."

"I'd do more than interview them if I got the chance," she said, rubbing her hands gleefully together.

"How about a swap then? You take the team and I'll run with the burglaries."

"Ha. Good try, Josh. But I don't think so."

I left the office at two-thirty. The training ground for the Warriors was on the other side of town and the afternoon was silvery and harsh. A white frost had formed on the window of my car. I scraped it all off before climbing inside and sat with the heater blasting to warm the interior and demist the window. Winter showed no sign of quitting. If anything, it was turning colder. In better weather, I would have walked from the office to the club. Woodbridge is a small town and it's possible to get from one side to the other in half an hour. But not in this weather.

Even in the car, with the heating on full, my fingers and toes were numb by the time I pulled up at the single-story club house. I hastened to the door and stepped inside.

The interior was as cold and depressing as the offices of the *Echo*. A long corridor stretched ahead with just a single window at the far end, leaking in gray light. There were several closed doors running off the corridor. It smelled of damp and drains and the unique stink of sweaty, sporty men, bringing back memories of the changing rooms at school. God, I despised it all back them. I was never a gifted athlete. The locker room was a place of depression and misery. Jibes from the bullying jocks still hurt. *Faggot. Gay boy. Arse bandit.* I was no longer that kid—being a keen runner and regular at the gym—but the emotional wounds of adolescence had left profound scars.

"Hello," I hollered. "Anyone here?"

About the Author

Thom Collins is the author of Closer by Morning, with Pride Publishing. His love of page turning thrillers began at an early age when his mother caught him reading the latest Jackie Collins book and promptly confiscated it, sparking a life-long love of raunchy novels.

Thom has lived in the North East of England his whole life. He grew up in Northumberland and now lives in County Durham with his husband and two cats. He loves all kinds of genre fiction, especially bonkbusters, thrillers, romance and horror. He is also a cookery book addict with far too many titles cluttering his shelves. When not writing he can be found in the kitchen trying out new recipes. He's a keen traveler but with a fear of flying that gets worse with age, but since taking his first cruise in 2013 he realized that sailing is the way to go.

Thom loves to hear from readers. You can find his contact information, website details and author profile page at http://www.pride-publishing.com.

PUBLISHING